THE HERMIT

Janet Bagley found her job strange, but un-cannily suited to a widow with a daughter to raise and no money—housekeeper to Charles Maxwell, a wealthy and reclusive writer in a remote house, a man who communicated with her only by letter, displaying only one evidence of human feeling, the presence of the young boy he allowed to share his home.

But eventually the strangeness grew too much for her, and she asked questions. She regretted that when the boy answered them. . . .

"You see, Mrs. Bagley, there isn't any Charles Maxwell. *I* am Charles Maxwell. I am eight years old, and I have been earning an excellent living as a writer for years. . . ."

THE FOURTH "R"

George O. Smith

A DELL BOOK

Published by
DELL PUBLISHING CO., INC.
1 Dag Hammarskjold Plaza
New York, New York 10017

ISBN: 0-440-13419-6

Reprinted by arrangement with the author.

Printed in the United States of America.

First Dell printing—April 1979

THE FOURTH
"R"

BOOK ONE:
FUTURE IMPROMPTU

CHAPTER ONE

James Quincy Holden was five years old.

His fifth birthday was not celebrated by the usual horde of noisy, hungry kids running wild in the afternoon. It started at seven, with cocktails. They were served by his host, Paul Brennan, to the celebrants, the boy's father and mother. The guest of honor sipped ginger ale and nibbled at canapés while he was presented with his gifts: A volume of Kipling's *Jungle Tales*, a Spitz Junior Planetarium, and a build-it-yourself kit containing parts for a geiger counter and an assortment of radioactive minerals to identify. Dinner was served at eight, the menu selected by Jimmy Holden—with the exception of the birthday cake and its five proud little candles which came as an anticipated surprise from his "Uncle" Paul Brennan.

After dinner, they listened to some music chosen by the boy, and the evening wound up with three rubbers of bridge. The boy won.

They left Paul Brennan's apartment just after eleven o'clock. Jimmy Holden was tired and pleasantly stuffed with good food. But he was stimulated by the party. So, instead of dropping off to sleep, he sat comfortably wedged between his father and mother, quietly lost in his own thoughts until the car was well out of town.

Then he said, "Dad, why did you make that sacrifice bid on the last hand?" Father and son had been partners.

"You're not concerned about losing the rubber, are you?" It had been the only rubber Jimmy lost.

"No. It's only a game," said Jimmy. "I'm just trying to understand."

His father gave an amused groan. "It has to do with the laws of probability and the theory of games," he said.

The boy shook his head. "Bridge," he said thoughtfully, "consists of creating a logical process of play out of a random distribution of values, doesn't it?"

"Yes, if you admit that your definition is a gross oversimplification. It would hardly be a game if everything could be calculated beforehand."

"But what's missing?"

"In any game there is the element of a calculated risk."

Jimmy Holden was silent for a half-mile thinking that one over. "How," he asked slowly, "can a risk be calculated?"

His father laughed. "In fine, it can't. Too much depends upon the personality of the individual."

"Seems to me," said Jimmy, "that there's not much point in making a bid against a distribution of values known to be superior. You couldn't hope to make it; Mother and Uncle Paul had the cards."

His father laughed again. "After a few more courses in higher mathematics, James, you'll begin to realize that some of the highest mathematics is aimed at predicting the unpredictable, or trying to lower the entropy of random behavior—"

Jimmy Holden's mother chuckled. "Now explain entropy," she said. "James, what your father has been failing to explain is really not subject to simple analysis. Who knows why any man will hazard his hard-earned money on the orientation of a pair of dice? No amount of education nor academic study will explain what drives a man. Deep inside, I suppose it is the same force that drives everybody. One man with four spades will take a chance to see if he can make five, and another man with directorships in three corporations will strive to make it four."

Jimmy's father chuckled. "Some families with one infant will try to make it two—"

"Not on your life!"

"—And some others are satisfied with what they've got," finished Jimmy Holden's father. "James, some men will avoid seeing what has to be done; some men will see it and do it and do no more; and a few men will see what has to be done, do it, and then look to the next inevitable problem created by their own act—"

A blinding flash of light cut a swath across the road, dazzling them. Around the curve ahead, a car careened wide over the white line. His mother reached for him, his father fought the wheel to avoid the crash. Jimmy Holden both heard and felt the sharp *Bang!* as the right front tire went. The steering wheel snapped through his father's hands by half a turn. There was a splintering crash as the car shattered its way through the retaining fence, then came a fleeting moment of breathless silence as if the entire universe had stopped still for a heartbeat.

Chaos! His mother's automatic scream, his father's oath, and the rending crash split the silence at once. The car bucked and flipped, the doors were slammed open and ripped off against a tree that went down. The car leaped in a skew turn and began to roll and roll, shedding metal and humans as it racketed down the ravine.

Jimmy felt himself thrown free in a tumbleturn that ended in a heavy thud.

When breath and awareness returned, he was lying in a depression filled with soft rotting leaves.

He was dazed beyond hurt. The initial shock and bewilderment oozed out of him, leaving him with a feeling of outrage, and a most peculiar sensation of being a spectator rather than an important part of the violent drama. It held an air of unreality, like a dream that the near-conscious sleeper recognizes as a dream and lives through it because he lacks the conscious will to direct it.

Strangely, it was as if there were three or more of him all thinking different things at the same time. He wanted his mother badly enough to cry. Another part of him said that she would certainly be at his side if she were able. Then a third section of his confused mind pointed out that if she did not come to him, it was because she herself was hurt deeply and couldn't.

A more coldly logical portion of his mind was urging him to get up and *do* something about it. They had passed a telephone booth on the highway; lying there whimpering wasn't doing anybody any good. This logical part of his confused mind did not supply the dime for the telephone slot nor the means of scaling the heights needed to insert the dime in the adult-altitude machine.

Whether the dazzle of mental activity was serial or simultaneous isn't important. The fact is that it was completely disorganized as to plan or program, it leaped from one subject to another until he heard the scrabble and scratch of someone climbing down the side of the ravine.

Any noise meant help. With relief, Jimmy tried to call out.

But with this arrival of help, afterfright claimed him. His mouth worked silently before a dead-dry throat and his muscles twitched in uncontrolled nervousness; he made neither sound nor motion. Again he watched with the unreal feeling of being a remote spectator. A cone of light from a flashlight darted about and it gradually seeped into Jimmy's shocked senses that this was a new arrival, picking his way through the tangle of brush, following the trail of ruin from the broken guard rail to the smashed car below.

The newcomer paused. The light darted forward to fall upon a crumpled mass of cloth.

With a toe, the stranger probed at crushed ribs. A pitifully feeble moan came from the broken rag doll that lay on the ground. The searcher knelt with his light close to peer into the bloody face, and, unbelieving, Jimmy Holden heard the voice of his mother straining to speak, "Paul—I—we—"

The voice died in a gurgle.

The man with the flashlight tested the flaccid neck by bending the head to one side and back sharply. He ended this inspection by letting the head fall back to the moist earth. It landed with a thud of finality.

The cold brutality of this stranger's treatment of his mother shocked Jimmy Holden into frantic outrage. The frozen cry for help changed into protesting anger; no one should be treated that—

"One!" muttered the stranger flatly.

Jimmy's burst of protest died in his throat and he watched, fascinated, as the stranger's light moved in a sweep forward to stop a second time. "And there's number two!" The callous horror was repeated. Hypnotically, Jimmy Holden watched the stranger test the temples and wrists and try a hand under his father's heart. He watched the stranger make a detailed inspection of the long slash that laid open the entire left abdomen and he saw the red that seeped but did not flow.

"That's that!" said the stranger with an air of finality. "Now—" and he stood up to swing his flashlight in widening circles, searching the area carefully.

Jimmy Holden did not sicken. He went cold. He froze as the dancing flashlight passed over his head, and relaxed partially when it moved away in a series of little jumps pausing to give a steady light for close inspection. The light swung around and centered on the smashed automobile. It was upside down, a ruin with one wheel still turning idly.

The stranger went to it, and knelt to peer inside. He pried ripped metal away to get a clear sight into the crushed interior. He went flat on his stomach and tried to penetrate the area between the crumpled car-top and the bruised ground, and he wormed his way in a circle all around the car, examining the wreck minutely.

The sound of a distant automobile engine became audible, and the searching man mumbled a curse. With haste he scrambled to his feet and made a quick inspection of the one wabbly-turning wheel. He stripped a few shards of rubber away, picked at something in the bent metal rim, and put whatever he found in his pocket. When his hand came from the pocket it held a packet of paper matches. With an ear cocked at the road above and the sound of the approaching car growing louder, the stranger struck one match and touched it to the deck of matches. Then with a callous gesture he tossed the flaring pack into a pool of spilled gasoline. The fuel went up in a blunt *whoosh!*

The dancing flames revealed the face of Jimmy Holden's "Uncle" Paul Brennan, his features in a mask that Jimmy Holden had never seen before.

With the determined air of one who knows that still another piece lies hidden, Paul Brennan started to beat back and forth across the trail of ruin. His light swept the ground like the brush of a painter, missing no spot. Slowly and deliberately he went, paying no attention to the creeping tongues of flame that crept along damp trails of spilled gasoline.

Jimmy Holden felt helplessly alone.

For "Uncle" Paul Brennan was the laughing uncle, the golden uncle; his godfather; the bringer of delightful gifts and the teller of fabulous stories. Classmate of his father and admirer of his mother, a friend to be trusted as he trusted his father and mother, as they trusted Paul Brennan. Jimmy Holden did not and could not understand, but he could feel the presence of menace. And so with the instinct of any trapped animal, he curled inward upon himself and cringed.

Education and information failed. Jimmy Holden had been told and told and instructed, and the words had been graven deep in his mind by the same fabulous machine that his father used to teach him his grammar and his vocabulary and his arithmetic and the horde of other things that made Jimmy Holden what he was: "If anything happens to us, you must turn to Paul Brennan!"

But nothing in his wealth of extraordinary knowledge covered the way to safety when the trusted friend turned fiend.

Shaken by the awful knowledge that all of his props had been kicked out from under him, now at last Jimmy Holden whimpered in helpless fright. Brennan turned towards the sound and began to beat his way through the underbrush.

Jimmy Holden saw him coming. It was like one of those dreams he'd had where he was unable to move, his muscles frozen, as some unknown horror stalked him. It could only end in a terrifying fall through cold space towards a tremendous lurch against the bedsprings that brought little comfort until his pounding heart came back to normal. But this was no dream; it was a known horror that stalked him, and it could not end as a dream ends. It was reality.

The horror was a close friend turned animal, and the end was more horrible because Jimmy Holden, like all other five-year-olds, had absolutely no understanding nor accurate grasp of the concept called *death*. He continued to whimper even though he realized that his fright was pointing him out to his enemy. And yet he had no real grasp of the concept *enemy*. He knew about pain; he had been hurt. But only by falls, simple misadventures, the needles of inoculation administered by his surgeon mother, a paddling for mischief by his engineer father.

But whatever unknown fate was coming was going to be worse than "hurt." It was frightful.

Then fate, assisted by Brennan's own act of trying to obliterate any possible evidence by fire, attracted a savior. The approaching car stopped on the road above and a voice called out, "Hello, down there!"

Brennan could not refuse to answer; his own car was in plain sight by the shattered retaining fence. He growled under his breath, but he called back, "Hello, the road! Go get the police!"

"Can we help?"

"Beyond help!" cried Brennan. "I'm all right. Get the cops!"

The car door slammed before it took off. Then came the unmistakable sounds of another man climbing down the ravine. A second flashlight swung here and there until the newcomer faced Brennan in the little circle of light.

"What happened?" asked the uninvited volunteer.

Brennan, whatever his thoughts, said in a voice filled with standard concern: "Blowout. Then everything went blooey."

"Anyone—I mean how many—?"

"Two dead," said Brennan, and then added because he had to, "and a little boy lost."

The stranger eyed the flames and shuddered. "In there?"

"Parents were tossed out. Boy's missing."

"Bad," said the stranger. "God, what a mess. Know 'em?"

"Holdens. Folks that live in the big old house on the hill. My best friend and his wife. I was following them home," lied Brennan glibly. "C'mon let's see if we can find the kid. What about the police?"

"Sent my wife. Telephone down the road."

Paul Brennan's reply carried no sound of disappointment over being interrupted. "Okay. Let's take a look. You take it that way, and I'll cover this side."

The little-boy mind did not need its extensive education to understand that Paul Brennan needed no more than a few seconds of unobserved activity, after which he could announce the discovery of the third death in a voice cracked with false grief.

Animal instinct took over where intelligence failed. The same force that caused Jimmy Holden to curl within himself now caused him to relax; help that could be trusted was now at hand. The muscles of his throat relaxed. He whimpered. The icy paralysis left his arms and legs; he kicked and flailed. And finally his nervous system succeeded in making their contact with his brain; the nerves carried the pain of his bumps and scratches, and Jimmy Holden began to hurt. His stifled whimper broke into a shuddering cry, which swiftly turned into sobbing hysteria.

He went out of control. Nothing, not even violence, would shake him back until his accumulation of shock upon shock had been washed away in tears.

The sound attracted both men. Side by side they beat through the underbrush. They reached for him and Jimmy turned toward the stranger. The man picked the lad out of the bed of soft rotting leaves, cradled him and stroked his head. Jimmy wrapped his small arms around the stranger's neck and held on for life.

"I'll take him," said Brennan, reaching out.

Jimmy's clutch on the stranger tightened.

"You won't pry him loose easily," chuckled the man. "I know. I've got a couple of these myself."

Brennan shrugged. "I thought perhaps—"

"Forget it," said the stranger. "Kid's had trouble. I'll carry him to the road, you take him from there."

"Okay."

Getting up the ravine was a job of work for the man who carried Jimmy Holden. Brennan gave a hand, aided with a lift, broke down brush, and of-

fered to take Jimmy now and again. Jimmy only
clung tighter, and the stranger waved Brennan away
with a quick shake of his head.

By the time they reached the road, sirens were
wailing on the road up the hill. Police, firemen, and
an ambulance swarmed over the scene. The firemen
went to work on the flaming car with practiced efficiency; the police clustered around Paul Brennan and
extracted from him a story that had enough truth in
it to sound completely convincing. The doctors from
the ambulance took charge of Jimmy Holden. Lacking any other accident victim, they went to work on
him with everything they could do.

They gave him mild sedation, wrapped him in a
warm blanket, and put him to bed on the cot in the
ambulance with two of them watching over him. In
the presence of so many solicitous strangers, Jimmy's
shock and fright diminished. The sedation took hold.
He dropped off in a light doze that grew less fitful as
time went on. By the time the official accident report
program was over, Jimmy Holden was fast asleep and
resting comfortably.

He did not hear Paul Brennan's suggestion that
Jimmy go home with him, to Paul Brennan's personal
physician, nor did Jimmy hear the ambulance atten-
dants turn away Brennan's suggestion with hard-
headed medical opinion. Brennan could hardly argue
with the fact that an accident victim would be better
off in a hospital under close observation. Shock demanded it, and there was the hidden possibility of in-
ternal injury or concussion to consider.

So Jimmy Holden awoke with his accident ten
hours behind him, and the good sleep had completed
the standard recuperative powers of the healthy child.
He looked around, collecting himself, and then
remembered the accident. He cringed a bit and took
another look and identified his surroundings as some
sort of a children's ward or dormitory.

He was in a crib.

He sat up angrily and rattled the gate of the crib. Putting James Quincy Holden in a baby's crib was an insult.

He stopped, because the noise echoed through the room and one of the younger patients stirred in sleep and moaned. Jimmy Holden sat back and remembered. The vacuum that was to follow the loss of his parents was not yet in evidence. They were gone and the knowledge made him unhappy, but he was not cognizant of the real meaning or emotion of grief. With almost the same feeling of loss he thought of the *Jungle Book* he would never read and the Spitz Planetarium he would never see casting its little star images on his bedroom ceiling. Burned and ruined, with the atomic energy kit—and he had hoped that he could use the kit to tease his father into giving him some education in radioactivity. He was old enough to learn—

Learn—?

No more, now that his father and mother were dead.

Some of the real meaning of his loss came to him then, and the growing knowledge that this first shocking loss meant the ultimate loss of everything was beginning to sink in.

He broke down and cried in the misery of his loss and his helplessness; ultimately his emotion began to cry itself out, and he began to feel resentment against his position. The animal desire to bite back at anything that moved did not last long, it focused properly upon the person of his tormentor. Then for a time, Jimmy Holden's imagination indulged in a series of little vignettes in which he scored his victory over Paul Brennan. These little playlets went through their own evolution, starting with physical victory reminiscent of his Jack-and-the-Beanstalk days to a more advanced triumph of watching Paul Brennan led away in handcuffs whilst the District Attor-

ney scanned the sheaf of indisputable evidence
provided by James Quincy Holden.

Somewhere along about this point in his fantasy, a
breath of the practical entered, and Jimmy began to
consider the more sensible problem of what sort of information this sheaf of evidence would contain.

Still identifying himself with the books he knew,
Jimmy Holden had progressed from the fairy story—
where the villain was evil for no more motive than to
provide menace to the hero—to his more advanced
books, where the villain did his evil deeds for the logical motive of personal gain.

Well, what had Paul Brennan to gain?

Money, for one thing—he would be executor of the
Holden Estate. But there wasn't enough to justify killing. Revenge? For what? Jealousy? For whom? Hate?
Envy? Jimmy Holden glossed the words quickly, for
they were no more than words that carried definitions
that did not really explain them. He could read with
the facility of an adult, but a book written for a so-
phisticated audience went over his head.

No, there was only one possible thing of apprecia-
ble value; the one thing that Paul Brennan hoped to
gain was the device over which they had worked
through all the long years to perfect: The Holden
Electromechanical Educator! Brennan wanted it
badly enough to murder for its possession!

And with a mind and ingenuity far beyond his
years, Jimmy Holden knew that he alone was the
most active operator in this vicious drama. It was not
without shock that he realized that he himself could
still be killed to gain possession of his fabulous
machine. For only with all *three* Holdens dead could
Paul Brennan take full and unquestioned possession.

With daylight clarity he knew what he had to do.
In a single act of destruction he could simultaneously
foil Paul Brennan's plan and ensure his own life.

Permanently installed in Jimmy Holden's brain by

the machine itself were the full details of how to re-create it. Indelibly he knew each wire and link, lever and coil, section by section and piece by piece. It was incomprehensible information, about in the same way that the printing press "knows" the context of its metal plate. Step by step he could rebuild it once he had the means of procuring the parts, and it would work even though he had not the foggiest notion (now) of what the various parts did.

So if the delicate heart of his father's machine were utterly destroyed, Paul Brennan would be extremely careful about preserving the life of James Quincy Holden.

He considered his position and what he knew:

Physically, he was a five-year-old. He stood forty-one inches tall and weighed thirty-nine pounds. A machinist's hammer was a two-handed tool and a five-pound sack of sugar was a burden. Doorknobs and latches were a problem in manipulation. The ne-gotiation of a swinging door was a feat of muscular engineering. Electric light switches were placed at a tiptoe reach because, naturally, everything in the adult world is designed by the adults for the con-venience of adults. This makes it difficult for the child who has no adult to do his bidding.

Intellectually, Jimmy Holden was something else.

Reverting to a curriculum considered sound prior to Mr. Dewey's often-questionable and more often misused programs of schooling, Jimmy's parents had trained and educated their young man quite well in the primary informations of fact. He read with facil-ity and spoke with a fine vocabulary—although no amount of intellectual training could make his voice change until his glands did. His knowledge of history, geography and literature were good, because he'd used them to study reading. He was well into plane geometry and had a smattering of algebra, and there had been a pause due to a parental argument as to the advisability of his memorizing a table of six-place logarithms via the Holden machine.

Extra-curricularly, Jimmy Holden had acquired snippets, bits, and wholesale chunks of a number of the arts and sciences and other aggregations of information both pertinent and trivial for one reason or another. As an instance, he had absorbed an entire bridge book by Charles Goren just to provide a fourth to sit in with his parents and Paul Brennan.

Consequently, James Holden had in data the education of a boy of about sixteen, and in other respects, much more.

He escaped from the hospital simply because no one ever thought that a five-year-old boy would have enough get-up-and-go to climb out of his crib, rummage a nearby closet, dress himself, and then calmly walk out. The clothing of a cocky teen-ager would have been impounded and his behavior watched.

They did not miss him for hours. He went, taking the little identification card from its frame at the foot of his bed—and that ruined the correlation between tag and patient.

By the time an overworked nurse stopped to think and finally asked, "Kitty, are you taking care of the little boy in Bed 6 over in 219?" and received the answer, "No, aren't you?" Jimmy Holden was trudging up the hill towards his home. Another hour went by with the two worried nurses surreptitiously searching the rest of the hospital in the simple hope that he had wandered away and could be restored before it came to the attention of the officials. By the time they gave up and called in other nurses (who helped them in their anxiety to conceal) Jimmy was entering his home.

Each succeeding level of authority was loath to report the truth to the next higher up.

By the time the general manager of the hospital forced himself to call Paul Brennan, Jimmy Holden was demolishing the last broken bits of disassembled subassemblies he had smashed from the heart-circuit of the Holden Electromechanical Educator. He was most thorough. Broken glass went into the refuse buckets, bent metal was buried in the garden, inflammables were incinerated, and meltables and fusibles slagged down in ashes that held glass, bottle, and empty tin-can in an unrecognizable mass. He left a gaping hole in the machine that Brennan could not fill—nor could any living man fill it now but James Quincy Holden.

And only when this destruction was complete did Jimmy Holden first begin to understand his father's statement about the few men who see what has to be done, do it, *and then* look to the next inevitable problem created by their own act.

It was late afternoon by the time Jimmy had his next moves figured out. He left the home he'd grown up in, the home of his parents, of his own babyhood. He'd wandered through it for the last time, touching this and saying goodbye to that. He was certain that he would never see his things again, nor the house itself, but the real vacuum of his loss hadn't yet started to form. The concepts of "never" and "forever" were merely words that had no real impact.

So was the word "Farewell."

But once his words were said, Jimmy Holden made his small but confident way to the window of a railroad ticket agent.

CHAPTER TWO

You are a ticket agent, settled in the routine of your job. From nine to five-thirty, five days a week, you see one face after another. There are cheerful faces, sullen faces, faces that breathe garlic, whiskey, chewing gum, toothpaste and tobacco fumes. Old faces, young faces, dull faces, scarred faces, clear faces, plain faces and faces so plastered with makeup that their nature can't be seen at all. They bark place-names at you, or ask pleasantly about the cost of round-trip versus one-way tickets to Chicago or East Burlap. You deal with them and then you wait for the next.

Then one afternoon, about four o'clock, a face barely visible over the edge of the marble counter looks up at you with a boy's cheerful freckled smile. You have to stand up in order to see him. You smile, and he grins at you. Among his belongings is a little leather suitcase, kid's size, but not a toy. He is standing on it. Under his arm is a collection of comic books, in one small fist is the remains of a candy bar and in the other the string of a floating balloon.

"Well, young man, where to? Paris? London? Maybe Mars?"

"No, sir," comes the piping voice, "Roun-tree."

"Roundtree? Yes, I've heard of that metropolis," you reply. You look over his head, there aren't any other customers in line behind him so you don't mind passing the time of day. "Round-trip or one-way?"

"One-way," comes the quick reply.

This brings you to a slow stop. He does not giggle

nor prattle, nor launch into a long and involved explanation with halting, dependent clauses. This one knows what he wants and how to ask for it. Quite a little man!

"How old are you, young fellow?"

"I was five years old yesterday."

"What's your name?"

"I'm James Holden."

The name does not ring any bells—because the morning newspaper is purchased for its comic strips, the bridge column, the crossword puzzle, and the latest dope on love-nest slayings, peccadilloes of the famous, the cheesecake photo of the inevitable actress-leaving-for-somewhere, and the full page photograph of the latest death-on-the-highway debacle. You look at the picture but you don't read the names in the caption, so you don't recognize the name, and you haven't been out of your little cage since lunchtime and Jimmy Holden was not missing then. So you go on:

"So you're going to go to Roundtree."

"Yessir."

"That costs a lot of money, young Mister Holden."

"Yessir." Then this young man hands you an envelope; the cover says, typewritten: *Ticket Clerk, Midland Railroad.*

A bit puzzled, you open the envelope and find a five-dollar bill folded in a sheet of manuscript paper. The note says:

Ticket Clerk
Midland Railroad
Dear Sir:
    This will introduce my son, James Holden. As a birthday present, I am sending him for a visit to his grandparents in Roundtree, and to make the adventure complete, he will travel alone. Pass the word along to keep an eye on him

but don't step in unless he gets into trouble. Ask the dining car steward to see that he eats dinner on something better than candy bars.

Otherwise, he is to believe that he is making this trip completely on his own.

Sincerely, Louis Holden.

PS: Divide the change from this five dollars among you as tips. L.H.

And so you look down at young Mister Holden and get a feeling of vicarious pleasure. You stamp his ticket and hand it to him with a gesture. You point out the train-gate he is to go through, and you tell him that he is to sit in the third railroad car. As he leaves, you pick up the telephone and call the station-master, the conductor, and since you can't get the dining-car steward directly, you charge the conductor with passing the word along.

Then you divide the change. Of the two-fifty, you extract a dollar, feeling that the Senior Holden is a cheapskate. You slip the other buck and a half into an envelope, ready for the conductor's hand. He'll think Holden Senior is more of a cheapskate, and by the time he extracts his cut, the dining car steward will *know* that Holden Senior is a cheapskate. But—

Then a face appears at your window and barks, "Holyoke, Mass.," and your normal day falls back into shape.

The response of the people you tell about it varies all the way from outrage that anybody would let a kid of five go alone on such a dangerous mission to loud bragging that he, too, once went on such a journey, at four and a half, and didn't need a note.

But Jimmy Holden is gone from your window, and you won't know for at least another day that you've been suckered by a note painstakingly typewritten, letter by letter, by a five-year-old boy who has a most remarkable vocabulary.

Jimmy's trip to Roundtree was without incident. Actually, it was easy once he had hurdled the ticket-seller with his forged note and the five-dollar bill from the cashbox in his father's desk. His error in not making it a ten was minor; a larger tip would not have provided him with better service, because the train crew were happy to keep an eye on the adventurous youngster for his own small sake. Their mild resentment against the small tip was directed against the boy's father, not the young passenger himself.

He had one problem. The train was hardly out of the station before everybody on it knew that there was a five-year-old making a trip all by himself. Of course, he was not to be bothered, but everybody wanted to talk to him, to ask him how he was, to chatter endlessly at him. Jimmy did not want to talk. His experience in addressing adults was exasperating. That he spoke lucid English instead of babygab did not compel a rational response. Those who heard him speak made over him with the same effusive superiority that they used in applauding a golden-haired tot in high heels and a strapless evening gown sitting on a piano and singing, *Why Was I Born?* in a piping, uncertain-toned voice. It infuriated him.

So he immersed himself in his comic books. He gave his name politely every five minutes for the first fifty miles. He turned down offers of candy with, "Mommy says I mustn't before supper." And when dinnertime came he allowed himself to be escorted through the train by the conductor, because Jimmy knew that he couldn't handle the doors without help.

The steward placed a menu in front of him, and then asked carefully, "How much money do you want to spend, young man?"

Jimmy had the contents of his father's cashbox pinned to the inside of his shirt, and a five-dollar bill folded in a snap-top purse with some change in his shirt pocket. He could add with the best of them, but he did not want any more attention than he was absolutely forced to attract. So he fished out the snap-top purse and opened it to show the steward his five-dollar bill. The steward relaxed; he'd had a moment of apprehension that Holden Senior might have slipped the kid a half-dollar for dinner. (The steward had received a quarter for his share of the original two-fifty.)

Jimmy looked at the "Child's Dinner" menu and pointed out a plate: lamb chop and mashed potatoes. After that, dinner progressed without incident. Jimmy topped it off with a dish of ice cream.

The steward made change. Jimmy watched him carefully, and then said, "Daddy says I'm supposed to give you a tip. How much?"

The steward looked down, wondering how he could explain the standard dining car tip of fifteen or twenty percent of the bill. He took a swallow of air and picked out a quarter. "This will do nicely," he said and went off thankful that all people do not ask waiters how much they think they deserve for the service rendered.

Thus Jimmy Holden arrived in Roundtree and was observed and convoyed—but not bothered—off the train.

It is deplorable that adults are not as friendly and helpful to one another as they are to children; it might make for a more pleasant world. As Jimmy walked along the station platform at Roundtree, one of his former fellow-passengers walked beside him. "Where are you going, young man? Someone going to meet you, of course?"

"No, sir," said Jimmy. "I'm supposed to take a cab—"

"I'm going your way, why not ride along with me?"

"Sure it's all right?"

"Sure thing. Come along." Jimmy never knew that this man felt good for a week after he'd done his good turn for the year.

His grandfather opened the door and looked down

at him in complete surprise. "Why, Jimmy! What are you doing here? Who brought—"

His grandmother interrupted, "Come in! Come in! Don't just stand there with the door open!"

Grandfather closed the door firmly, grandmother knelt and folded Jimmy in her arms and crooned over him, "You poor darling. You brave little fellow. Donald," she said firmly to her husband, "go get a glass of warm milk and some cookies." She led Jimmy to the old-fashioned parlor and seated him on the sofa. "Now, Jimmy, you relax a moment and then you can tell me what happened."

Jimmy sighed and looked around. The house was old, and comfortably sturdy. It gave him a sense of refuge, of having reached a safe haven at last. The house was over-warm, and there was a musty smell of overaged furniture, old leather, and the pungence of mothballs. It seemed to generate a feeling of firm stability. Even the slightly stale air—there probably hadn't been a wide open window since the storm sashes were installed last autumn—provided a locked-in feeling that conversely meant that the world was locked out.

Grandfather brought in the glass of warmed milk and a plate of cookies. He sat down and asked, "What happened, Jimmy?"

"My mother and father are—"

"You eat your cookies and drink your milk," ordered his grandmother. "We know. That Mr. Brennan sent us a telegram."

It was slightly more than twenty-four hours since Jimmy Holden had blown out the five proud candles on his birthday cake and begun to open his fine presents. Now it all came back with a rush, and when it came back, nothing could stop it.

Jimmy never knew how very like a little boy of five he sounded that night. His speech was clear enough, but his troubled mind was too full to take the time to form his headlong thoughts into proper sentences. He could not pause to collect his thoughts into any chronology, so it came out going back and forth all in a single line, punctuated only by necessary pauses for the intake of breath. He was close to tears before he was halfway through, and by the time he came to the end he stopped in a sob and broke out crying.

His grandfather said, "Jimmy, aren't you exaggerating? Mr. Brennan isn't that sort of a man."

"He is too!" exploded Jimmy through his tears. "I saw him!"

"But—"

"Donald, this is no time to start cross-examining a child." She crossed the room and lifted him onto her lap; she stroked his head and held his cheek against her shoulder. His open crying subsided into deep sobs; from somewhere she found a handkerchief and made him blow his nose—once, twice, and then a deep thrice. "Get me a warm washcloth," she told her husband, and with it she wiped away his tears. The warmth soothed Jimmy more.

"Now," she said firmly, "before we go into this any more we'll have a good night's sleep."

The featherbed was soft and cozy. Like protecting mother-wings, it folded Jimmy into its bosom, and the warm softness drew out of Jimmy whatever remained of his stamina. Tonight he slept of weariness and exhaustion, not of the sedation given last night. Here he felt at home, and it was good.

And as tomorrows always had, tomorrow would take care of itself.

Jimmy Holden's father and mother first met over an operating table, dressed in the white sterility that leaves only the eyes visible. She wielded the trephine that laid the patient's brain bare, he kept track of the patient's life by observing the squiggles on the roll of graph paper that emerged from his encephalograph. She knew nothing of the craft of the delicate instrument-creator, and he knew even less of the craft of surgery. There had been a near-argument during the cleaning-up session after the operation; the near-argument ended when they both realized that neither of them understood a word of what the other was saying. So the near-argument became an animated discussion, the general meaning of which became clear: Brain surgeons should know more about the intricacies of electromechanics, and the designers of delicate, precision instrumentation should know more about the mass of human gray matter they were trying to measure.

They pooled their intellects and plunged into the problem of creating an encephalograph that would record the infinitesimal irregularities that were superimposed upon the great waves. Their operation became large; they bought the old structure on top of the hill and moved in, bag and baggage. They cohabited but did not live together for almost a year; Paul Brennan finally pointed out that Organized Society might permit a couple of geniuses to become research hermits, but Organized Society still took a dim view of cohabitation without a license. Besides, such messy arrangements always cluttered up the legal clarity of chattels, titles, and estates.

They married in a quiet ceremony about two years prior to the date that Louis Holden first identified the fine-line wave-shapes that went with determined ideas. When he recorded them and played them back, his brain re-traced its original line of thought, and he could not even make a mental revision of the way his thoughts were arranged. For two years Louis and Laura Holden picked their way slowly through this field; stumped at one point for several months because the machine was strictly a personal proposition. Recorded by one of them, the playback was clear to that one, but to the other it was wild gibberish—an inexplicable tangle of noise and colored shapes, odors and tastes both pleasant and nasty, and mingled sensations. It was five years after their marriage before they found success by engraving information in the brain by sitting, connected to the machine, and reading aloud, word for word, the information that they wanted.

It went by rote, as they had learned in childhood. It was the tiresome repetition of going over and over and over the lines of a poem or the numbers of the multiplication table until the pathway was a deeply trodden furrow in the brain. Forever imprinted, it was retained until death. Knowledge is stored by rote.

To accomplish this end, Louis Holden succeeded in violating all of the theories of instrumentation by developing a circuit that acted as a sort of reverberation chamber which returned the wave-shape played into it back to the same terminals without interference, and this single circuit became the very heart of the Holden Electromechanical Educator.

With success under way, the Holdens needed an intellectual guinea pig, a virgin mind, an empty storehouse to fill with knowledge. They planned a twenty-year program of research, to end by handing their machine to the world complete with its product and instructions for its use and a list of pitfalls to avoid.

The conception of James Quincy Holden was a most carefully-planned parenthood. It was not accomplished without love or passion. Love had come quietly, locking them together physically as they had been bonded intellectually. The passion had been deliberately provoked during the proper moment of Laura Holden's cycle of ovulation. This scientific approach to procreation was no experiment, it was the foregone-conclusive act to produce a component absolutely necessary for the completion of their long program of research. They happily left to Nature's Choice the one factor they could not control, and planned to accept an infant of either sex with equal welcome. They loved their little boy as they loved one another, rejoiced with him, despaired with him, and made their own way with success and mistake, and succeeded in bringing Jimmy to five years of age quite normal except for his education.

Now, proficiency in brain surgery does not come at an early age, nor does world-wide fame in the field of delicate instrumentation. Jimmy's parents were over forty-five on the date of his birth.

Jimmy's grandparents were, then, understandably aged seventy-eight and eighty-one.

The old couple had seen their life, and they knew it for what it was. They arose each morning and faced the day knowing that there would be no new problem, only recurrence of some problem long solved. Theirs was a comfortable routine, long gone was their spirit of adventure, the pleasant notions of trying something a new and different way. At their age, they were content to take the easiest and the simplest way of doing what they thought to be Right. Furthermore, they had lived long enough to know that no equitable decision can be made by listening to only one side of any argument.

While young Jimmy was polishing off a platter of scrambled eggs the following morning, Paul Brennan arrived. Jimmy's fork stopped in midair at the sound of Brennan's voice in the parlor.

"You called him," he said accusingly.

Grandmother Holden said, "He's your legal guardian, James."

"But—I don't—can't—"

"Now, James, your father and mother knew best."

"But they didn't know about Paul Brennan. I won't go!"

"You must."

"I won't!"

"James," said Grandmother Holden quietly, "you can't stay here."

"Why not?"

"We're not prepared to keep you."

"Why not?"

Grandmother Holden despaired. How could she make this youngster understand that eighty is not an age at which to embark upon the process of raising a five-year-old to maturity?

From the other room, Paul Brennan was explaining his side as he'd given it to the police. "—Forgot the land option that had to be signed. So I took off after them and drove fast enough to catch up. I was only a couple of hundred yards behind when it happened."

"He's a liar!" cried Jimmy Holden.

"That's not a nice thing to say."

"It's true!"

"Jimmy!" came the reproachful tone.

"It's true!" he cried.

His grandfather and Paul Brennan came into the kitchen. "Ah, Jimmy," said Paul in a soothing voice, "why did you run off? You had everybody worried."

"You did! You lie! You—"

"James!" snapped his grandfather. "Stop that talk at once!"

"Be easy with him, Mr. Holden. He's upset. Jimmy, let's get this settled right now. What did I do and how do I lie?"

"Oh, please Mr. Brennan," said his grandmother. "This isn't necessary."

"Oh, but it is. It is very important. As the legal guardian of young James, I can't have him harboring some suspicion as deep as this. Come on, Jimmy. Let's talk it out right now. What did I do and how am I lying?"

"You weren't behind. You forced us off the road."

"How could he, young man?" demanded Grandfather Holden.

"I don't know, but he did."

"Wait a moment, sir," said Brennan quietly. "It isn't going to be enough to force him into agreement. He's got to see the truth for itself, of his own con-

struction from the facts. Now, Jimmy, where was I
when you left my apartment?"

"You—you were there."

"And didn't I say—"

"One moment," said Grandfather Holden. "Don't
lead the witness."

"Sorry. James, what did I do?"

"You—" then a long pause.

"Come on, Jimmy."

"You shook hands with my father."

"And then?"

"Then you—kissed my mother on the cheek."

"And then, again?"

"And then you carried my birthday presents down
and put them in the car."

"Now, Jimmy, how does your father drive? Fast or
slow?"

"Fast."

"So now, young man, you tell me how I could go
back up to my apartment, get my coat and hat, get
my car out of the garage, and race to the top of that
hill so that I could turn around and come at you
around that curve? Just tell me that, young man."

"I—don't know—how you did it."

"It doesn't make sense, does it?"

"—No—"

"Jimmy, I'm trying to help you. Your father and I
were fraternity brothers in college. I was best man at
your parents' wedding. I am your godfather. Your
folks were taken away from both of us—and I'm
hoping to take care of you as if you were mine." He
turned to Jimmy's grandparents. "I wish to God that
I could find the driver of that other car. He didn't hit
anybody, but he's as guilty of a hit-and-run offence as
the man who does. If I ever find him, I'll have him in
jail until he rots!"

"Jimmy," pleaded his grandmother, "can't you see?
Mr. Brennan is only trying to help. Why would he do
the evil thing you say he did?"

"Because—" and Jimmy started to cry. The utter futility of trying to make people believe was too much to bear.

"Jimmy, please stop it and be a man," said Brennan. He put a hand on Jimmy's shoulder. Jimmy flung it aside with a quick twist and a turn. "Please, Jimmy," pleaded Brennan. Jimmy left his chair and buried his face in a corner of the wall.

"Jimmy, believe me," pleaded Brennan. "I'm going to take you to live in your old house, among your own things. I can't replace your folks, but I can try to be as close to your father as I know how. I'll see you through everything, just as your mother and father want me to."

"No!" exploded Jimmy through a burst of tears.

Grandfather Holden grunted. "This is getting close to the tantrum stage," he said. "And the only way to deal with a tantrum is to apply the flat of the hand to the round of the bottom."

"Please," smiled Brennan. "He's a pretty shaken youngster. He's emotionally hurt and frightened, and he wants to strike out and hurt something back."

"I think he's done enough of that," said Grandfather Holden. "When Louis tossed one of these fits of temper where he wouldn't listen to any reason, we did as we saw fit anyway and let him kick and scream until he got tired of the noise he made."

"Let's not be rough," pleaded Jimmy's grandmother. "He's just a little boy, you know."

"If he weren't so little he'd have better sense," snapped Grandfather.

"James," said Paul Brennan quietly, "do you see you're making trouble for your grandparents? Haven't we enough trouble as it is? Now, young man, for the last time, will you walk or will you be carried? Whichever, Jimmy, we're going back home!"

James Holden gave up. "I'll go," he said bitterly, "but I hate you."

"He'll be all right," promised Brennan. "I swear it!"

"Please, Jimmy, be good for Mr. Brennan," pleaded his grandmother. "After all, it's for your own good." Jimmy turned away, bewildered, hurt and silent. He stubbornly refused to say goodbye to his grandparents.

He was trapped in the world of grown-ups that believed a lying adult before they would even consider the truth of a child.

CHAPTER THREE

The drive home was a bitter experience. Jimmy was sullen, and very quiet. He refused to answer any question and he made no reply to any statement. Paul Brennan kept up a running chatter of pleasantries, of promises and plans for their future, and just enough grief to make it sound honest. Had Paul Brennan actually been as honest as his honeyed tones said he was, no one could have continued to accuse him. But no one is more difficult to fool than a child—even a normal child. Paul Brennan's protestations simply made Jimmy Holden bitter.

He sat silent and unhappy in the far corner of the front seat all the way home. In his mind was a nameless threat, a dread of what would come once they were inside—either inside of Paul Brennan's apartment or inside of his own home—with the door locked against the outside world.

But when they arrived, Paul Brennan continued his sympathetic attitude. To Jimmy it was sheer hypocrisy; he was not experienced enough to know that a person can commit an act and then convince himself that he hadn't.

"Jimmy," said Brennan softly, "I have not the faintest notion of punishment. None whatsoever. You ruined your father's great invention. You did that because you thought it was right. Someday when you change your mind and come to believe in me, I'll ask you to replace it because I know you can. But understand me, young man, I shall not ask you until you make the first suggestion yourself!"

Jimmy remained silent.

"One more thing," said Brennan firmly. "Don't try that stunt with the letter to the station agent again. It won't work twice. Not in this town nor any other for a long, long time. I've made a sort of family-news item out of it which hit a lot of daily papers. It'll also be in the company papers of all the railroads and buslines, how Mr. What's-his-name at the Midland Railroad got suckered by a five-year-old running away from home. Understand?"

Jimmy understood but made no sign.

"Then in September we'll start you in school," said Brennan.

This statement made no impression upon young James Holden whatsoever. He had no intention of enduring this smothering by overkindness any longer than it took him to figure out how to run away, and where to run to. It was going to be a difficult thing. Cruel treatment, torture, physical harm were one thing; this act of being a deeply-concerned guardian was something else. A twisted arm he could complain about, a bruise he could show, the scars of lashing would give credence to his tale. But who would listen to any complaint about too much kindness?

Six months of this sort of treatment and Jimmy Holden himself would begin to believe that his parents were monsters, coldly stuffing information in the head of an infant instead of letting him grow through a normal childhood. A year, and Jimmy Holden would be re-creating his father's reverberation circuit out of sheer gratitude. He'd be cajoled into signing his own death-warrant.

But where can a five-year-old hide? There was no appeal to the forces of law and order. They would merely pop him into a squad car and deliver him to his guardian.

Law and order were out. His only chance was to

lose himself in some gray hinterland where there were so many of his own age that no one could keep track of them all. Whether he would succeed was questionable. But until he tried, he wouldn't know, and Jimmy was desperate enough to try anything.

He attended the funeral services with Paul Brennan. But while the pastor was invoking Our Heavenly Father to accept the loving parents of orphaned James, James the son left the side of his "Uncle" Paul Brennan, who knelt in false piety with his eyes closed.

Jimmy Holden had with him only his clothing and what was left of the wad of paper money from his father's cashbox still pinned to the inside of his shirt.

This time Jimmy did not ride in style. Burlap sacks covered him when night fell; they dirtied his clothing and the bottom of the freight car scuffed his shoes. For eighteen hours he hid in the jolting darkness, not knowing and caring less where he was going, so long as it was away!

He was hungry and thirsty by the time the train first began to slow down. It was morning—somewhere. Jimmy looked furtively out of the slit at the edge of the door to see that the train was passing through a region of cottages dusted black by smoke, through areas of warehouse and factory, through squalor and filth and slum; and vacant lots where the spread of the blight area had been so fast that the outward improvement had not time to build. Eventually the scene changed to solid areas of railroad track, and the trains parked there thickened until he could no longer see the city through them.

Ultimately the train stopped long enough for Jimmy to squeeze out through the slit at the edge of the door.

The train went on and Jimmy was alone in the middle of some huge city. He walked the noisome sidewalk trying to decide what he should do next. Food was of high importance, but how could he get it without attracting attention to himself? He did not know. But finally he reasoned that a hot dog wagon would probably take cash from a youngster without asking embarrassing questions, so long as the cash wasn't anything larger than a five-dollar bill.

He entered the next one he came to. It was dirty; the windows held several years' accumulation of cooking grease, but the aroma was terrific to a young animal who'd been without food since yesterday afternoon.

The counterman did not like kids, but he put away his dislike at the sight of Jimmy's money. He grunted when Jimmy requested a dog, tossed one on the grill and went back to reading his newspaper until some inner sense told him it was cooked. Jimmy finished it still hungry and asked for another. He finished a third and washed down the whole mass with a tall glass of highly watered orange juice. The counterman took his money and was very careful about making the right change; if this dirty kid had swiped the five-spot, it could be the counterman's problem of explaining to someone why he had overcharged. Jimmy's intelligence told him that countermen in a joint like this didn't expect tips, so he saved himself that hurdle. He left the place with a stomach full of food that only the indestructible stomach of a five-year-old could handle and now, fed and reasonably content, Jimmy began to seek his next point of contact.

He had never been in a big city before. The sheer number of human beings that crowded the streets surpassed his expectations. The traffic was not personally terrifying, but it was so thick that Jimmy Holden wondered how people drove without colliding. He knew about traffic lights and walked with the green, staying out of trouble. He saw groups of small children playing in the streets and in the empty lots. Those not much older than himself were attending school.

He paused to watch a group of children his own

age trying to play baseball with a ragged tennis ball and the handle from a broom. It was a helter-skelter game that made no pattern but provided a lot of fun and screaming. He was quite bothered by a quarrel that came up; two of his own age went at one another with tiny fists flying, using words that Jimmy hadn't learned from his father's machine.

He wondered how he might join them in their game. But they paid him no attention, so he didn't try.

At lunchtime Jimmy consumed another collection of hot dogs. He continued to meander aimlessly through the city until schooltime ended, then he saw the streets and vacant lots fill with older children playing games with more pattern to them. It was a new world he watched, a world that had not been a part of his education. The information he owned was that of the school curriculum; it held nothing of the daily business of growing up. He knew the general rules of big-league baseball, but the kid-business of stickball did not register.

He was at a complete loss. It was sheer chance and his own tremendous curiosity that led him to the edge of a small group that were busily engaged in the odd process of trying to jack up the front of a car.

It wasn't a very good jack; it should have had the weight of a full adult against the handle. The kids strained and put their weight on the jack, but the handle wouldn't budge though their feet were off the ground.

Here was the place where academic information would be useful—and the chance for an "in." Jimmy shoved himself into the small group and said, "Get a longer handle."

They turned on him suspiciously.

"Whatcha know about it?" demanded one, shoving his chin out.

"Get a longer handle," repeated Jimmy. "Go ahead, get one."

"G'wan—"

"Wait, Moe. Maybe—"

"Who's he?"

"I'm Jimmy."

"Jimmy who?"

"Jimmy—James." Academic information came up again. "Jimmy. Like the jimmy you use on a window."

"Jimmy James. Any relation to Jesse James?"

James Quincy Holden now told his first whopper. "I," he said, "am his grandson."

The one called Moe turned to one of the younger ones. "Get a longer handle," he said.

While the younger one went for something to use as a longer handle, Moe invited Jimmy to sit on the curb. "Cigarette?" invited Moe.

"I don't smoke," said Jimmy.

"Sissy?"

Adolescent-age information looking out through five-year-old eyes assayed Moe. Moe was about eight, maybe even nine; taller than Jimmy but no heavier. He had a longer reach, which was an advantage that Jimmy did not care to hazard. There was no sure way to establish physical superiority; Jimmy was uncertain whether any show of intellect would be welcome.

"No," he said. "I'm no sissy. I don't like 'em."

Moe lit a cigarette and smoked with much gesturing and flickings of ashes and spitting at a spot on the pavement. He was finished when the younger one came back with a length of water pipe that would fit over the handle of the jack.

The car went up with ease. Then came the business of removing the hubcap and the struggle to loose the lugbolts. Jimmy again suggested the application of the length of pipe. The wheel came off.

"C'mon, Jimmy," said Moe. "We'll cut you in."

"Sure," nodded Jimmy Holden, willing to see what came next so long as it did not have anything to do with Paul Brennan. Moe trundled the car wheel down the street, steering it with practiced hands. A block down and a block around that corner, a man with a three-day growth of whiskers stopped a truck with a very dirty license plate. Moe stopped and the man jumped out of the truck long enough to heave the tire and wheel into the back.

The man gave Moe a handful of change which Moe distributed among the little gang. Then he got in the truck beside the driver and waved for Jimmy to come along.

"What's that for?" demanded the driver.

"He's a smarty pants," said Moe. "A real good one."

"Who're you?"

"Jimmy—James."

"What'cha do, kid?"

"What?"

"Moe, what did this kid sell you?"

"You and your rusty jacks," grunted Moe. "Jimmy James here told us how to put a long hunk of pipe on the handle."

"Jimmy James, who taught you about leverage?" demanded the driver suspiciously.

Jimmy Holden believed that he was in the presence of an educated man. "Archimedes," he said solemnly, giving it the proper pronunciation.

The driver said to Moe, "Think he's all right?"

"He's smart enough."

"Who're your parents, kid?"

Jimmy Holden realized that this was a fine time to tell the truth, but properly diluted to taste. "My folks are dead," he said.

"Who you staying with?"

"No one."

The driver of the truck eyed him cautiously for a moment. "You escaped from an orphan asylum?"

"Uh-huh," lied Jimmy.

"Where?"

"Ain't saying."

"Wise, huh?"

"Don't want to get sent back," said Jimmy.

"Got a flop?"

"Flop?"

"Place to sleep for the night."

"No."

"Where'd you sleep last night?"

"Boxcar."

"Bindlestiff, huh?" roared the man with laughter.

"No, sir," said Jimmy. "I've no bindle."

The man's roar of laughter stopped abruptly. "You're a pretty wise kid," he said thoughtfully.

"I told y' so," said Moe.

"Shut up," snapped the man. "Kid, do you want a flop for the night?"

"Sure."

"Okay. You're in."

"What's your name?" asked Jimmy.

"You call me Jake. Short for Jacob. Er—here's the place."

The "Place" had no other name. It was a junkyard. In it were car parts, wrecks with parts undamaged, whole motors rusting in the air, axles, wheels, differential assemblies and transmissions from a thousand cars of a thousand different parentages. Hubcaps abounded in piles sorted to size and shape. Jake drove the little pickup truck into an open shed. The tire and wheel came from the back and went immediately into place on a complicated gadget. In a couple of minutes, the tire was off the wheel and the inner tube was out of the casing. Wheel, casing, and inner tube all went into three separate storage piles.

Not only a junkyard, but a stripper's paradise. Bring a hot car in here and in a few hours no one could find it. Its separated parts would be sold piece by piece and week by week as second-hand replacements.

Jake said, "Dollar-fifty."

"Two," said Moe.

"One seventy-five."

"Two."

"Go find it and put it back."

"Gimme the buck-six," grunted Moe. "Pretty cheap for a good shoe, a wheel, and a sausage."

"Bring it in alone next time, and I'll slip you two-fifty. That gang you use costs, too. Now scram, Jimmy James and I got business to talk over."

"He taking over?"

"Don't talk stupid. I need a spotter. You're too old, Moe. And if he's any good, you gotta promotion coming."

"And if he ain't?"

"Don't come back!"

Moe eyed Jimmy Holden. "Make it good—Jimmy." There was malice in Moe's face.

Jake looked down at Jimmy Holden. With precisely the same experienced technique he used to estimate the value of a car loaded with road dirt, rust, and collision-smashed fenders, Jake stripped the child of the dirty clothing, the scuffed shoes, the mussed hair, and saw through to the value beneath. Its price was one thousand dollars, offered with no questions asked for information that would lead to the return of one James Quincy Holden to his legal guardian.

It wasn't magic on Jake's part. Paul Brennan had instantly offered a reward. And Jake made it his business to keep aware of such matters.

How soon, wondered Jake, might the ante be raised to two Gee? Five? And in the meantime, if things panned, Jimmy could be useful as a spotter.

"You afraid of that Moe punk, Jimmy?"

"No sir."

"Good, but keep an eye on him. He'd sell his mother for fifty cents clear profit—seventy-five if he had to split the deal. Now, kid, do you know anything about spotting?"

"No sir."

"Hungry?"

"Yes sir."

"All right. Come on in and we'll eat. Do you like Mulligan?"

"Yes sir."

"Good. You and me are going to get along."

Inside of the squalid shack, Jake had a cozy set-up. The filth that he encouraged out in the junkyard was not tolerated inside his shack. The dividing line was halfway across the edge of the door; the inside was as clean, neat, and shining as the outside was squalid.

"You'll sleep here," said Jake, waving towards a small bedroom with a single twin bunk. "You'll make yer own bed and take a shower every night—or out! Understand?"

"Yes sir."

"Good. Now, let's have chow, and I'll tell you about this spotting business. You help me, and I'll help you. One blab and back you go to where you came from. Get it?"

"Yes sir."

And so, while the police of a dozen cities were scouring their beats for a homeless, frightened five-year-old, Jimmy Holden slept in a comfortable bed in a clean room, absolutely disguised by an exterior that looked like an abandoned manure shed.

CHAPTER FOUR

Jimmy discovered that he was admirably suited to the business of spotting. The "job turnover" was high because the spotter must be young enough to be allowed the freedom of the preschool age, yet be mature enough to follow orders.

The job consisted of meandering through the streets of the city, in the aimless patterns of youth, while keeping an eye open for parked automobiles with the ignition keys still in their locks.

Only a very young child can go whooping through the streets bumping pedestrians, running wildly, or walking from car to car twiggling each door handle and peering inside as if he were imitating a door-to-door salesman, occasionally making a minor excursion in one shop door and out the other.

He takes little risk. He merely spots the target. He reports that there is such-and-such a car parked so-and-so, after which he goes on to spot the next target. The rest of the business is up to the men who do the actual stealing.

Jimmy's job-training program took only one morning. That same afternoon he went to work for Jake's crew.

Jake's experience with kids had been no more than so-so promising. He used them because they were better than nothing. He did not expect them to stay long; they were gobbled up by the rules of compulsory education just about the age when they could be counted upon to follow orders.

He felt about the same with Jimmy Holden; the "missing person" report stated that one of the most prominent factors in the lad's positive identification was his high quality of speech and his superior intelligence. (This far Paul Brennan had to go, and he had divulged the information with great reluctance.)

But though Jake needed a preschool child with intelligence, he did not realize the height of Jimmy Holden's.

It was obvious to Jimmy on the second day that Jake's crew was not taking advantage of every car spotted. One of them had been a "natural" to Jimmy's way of thinking. He asked Jake about it: "Why didn't you take the sea-green Ford in front of the corner store?"

"Too risky."

"Risky?"

Jake nodded. "Spotting isn't risky, Jimmy. But picking the car up is. There is a very dangerous time when the driver is a sitting duck. From the moment he opens the car door he is in danger. Sitting in the chance of getting caught, he must start the car, move it out of the parking space into traffic, and get under way and gone before he is safe."

"But the sea-green Ford was sitting there with its engine running!"

"Meaning," nodded Jake, "that the driver pulled in and made a fast dash into the store for a newspaper or a pack of cigarettes."

"I understand. Your man could get caught. Or," added Jimmy thoughtfully, "the owner might even take his car away before we got there."

Jake nodded. This one was going to make it easy for him.

As the days wore on, Jimmy became more selective. He saw no point in reporting a car that wasn't going to be used. An easy mark wedged between two other cars couldn't be removed with ease. A car parked in front of a parking meter with a red flag was dangerous, it meant that the time was up and the driver should be getting nervous about it. A man who came shopping along the street to find a meter with some time left by the former driver was obviously looking for a quick-stop place—whereas the man who fed the meter to its limit was a much better bet.

Jake, thankful for what Fate had brought him, now added refinements of education. Cars parked in front of supermarkets weren't safe; the owner might be standing just inside the big plate glass window. The car parked hurriedly just before the opening of business was likely to be a good bet because people are careless about details when they are hurrying to punch the old time clock.

Jake even closed down his operations during the calculated danger periods, but he made sure to tell Jimmy Holden why.

From school-closing to dinnertime Jimmy was allowed to do as he pleased. He found it hard to enjoy playing with his contemporaries, and Jake's explanation about dangerous times warned Jimmy against joining Moe and his little crew of thieves. Jimmy would have enjoyed helping in the stripping yard, but he had not the heft for it. They gave him little messy jobs to do that grimed his hands and made Jake's stern rule of cleanliness hard to achieve. Jimmy found it easier to avoid such jobs than to scrub his skin raw.

One activity he found to his ability was the cooking business.

Jake was a stew-man, a soup-man, a slum-gullion man. The fellows who roamed in and out of Jake's Place dipped their plate of slum from the pot and their chunk of bread from the loaf and talked all through this never-started and never-ended lunch. With the delicacy of his "inside" life, Jake knew the value of herbs and spices and he was a hard taskmaster. But inevitably, Jimmy learned the routine of brewing a bucket of slum that suited Jake's taste, after which Jimmy was now and then permitted to take on the more demanding job of cooking the steaks and chops that made their final evening meal.

Jimmy applied himself well, for the knowledge was going to be handy. More important, it kept him from the jobs that grimed his hands.

He sought other pursuits, but Jake had never had a resident spotter before and the play-facilities provided were few. Jimmy took to reading—necessarily, the books that Jake read, that is, approximately equal parts of science fiction and girlie-girlie books. The science fiction he enjoyed; but he was not able to understand why he wasn't interested in the girlie books. So Jimmy read. Jake even went out of his way to find more science fiction for the lad.

Ultimately, Jimmy located a potential source of pleasure.

He spotted a car with a portable typewriter on the back seat. The car was locked and therefore no target, but it stirred his fancy. Thereafter he added a contingent requirement to his spotting. A car with a typewriter was more desirable than one without.

Jimmy went on to further astound Jake by making a list of what the customers were buying. After that he concentrated on spotting those cars that would provide the fastest sale for their parts.

It was only a matter of time; Jimmy spotted a car with a portable typewriter. It was not as safe a take as his others, but he reported it. Jake's driver picked it up and got it out in a squeak; the car itself turned up to be no great find.

Jimmy claimed the typewriter at once.

Jake objected: "No dice, Jimmy."

"I want it, Jake."

"Look, kid, I can sell it for twenty."

"But I want it."

Jake eyed Jimmy thoughtfully, and he saw two things. One was a thousand-dollar reward standing before him. The other was a row of prison bars.

Jake could only collect one and avoid the other by being very sure that Jimmy Holden remained grateful to Jake for Jake's shelter and protection.

He laughed roughly. "All right, Jimmy," he said. "You lift it and you can have it."

Jimmy struggled with the typewriter, and succeeded only because it was a new one made of the titanium-magnesium-aluminum alloys. It hung between his little knees, almost—but not quite—touching the ground.

"You have it," said Jake. He lifted it lightly and carried it into the boy's little bedroom.

Jimmy started after dinner. He picked out the letters with the same painful search he'd used in typing his getaway letter. He made the same mistakes he'd made before. It had taken him almost an hour and nearly fifty sheets of paper to compose that first note without an error; that was no way to run a railroad; now Jimmy was determined to learn the proper operation of this machine. But finally the jagged tack-tack—pause—tack-tack got on Jake's nerves.

Jake came in angrily. "You're wasting paper," he snapped. He eyed Jimmy thoughtfully. "How come with your education you don't know how to type?"

"My father wouldn't let me."

"Seems your father wouldn't let you do anything."

"He said that I couldn't learn until I was old enough to learn properly. He said I must not get into the habit of using the hunt-and-peck system, or I'd never get out of it."

"So what are you doing now?"

"My father is dead."

"And anything he said before doesn't count any more?"

"He promised me that he'd start teaching me as soon as my hands were big enough," said Jimmy soberly. "But he isn't here any more. So I've got to learn my own way."

Jake reflected. Jimmy was a superior spotter. He

was also a potential danger; the other kids played it as a game and didn't really realize what they were doing. This one knew precisely what he was doing, knew that it was wrong, and had the lucidity of speech to explain in full detail. It was a good idea to keep him content.

"If you'll stop that tap-tapping for tonight," promised Jake, "I'll get you a book tomorrow. Is it a deal?"

"You will?"

"I will if you'll follow it."

"Sure thing."

"And," said Jake, pushing his advantage, "you'll do it with the door closed so's I can hear this TV set."

"Yes sir."

Jake kept his word.

On the following afternoon, not only was Jimmy presented with one of the standard learn-it-yourself books on touch-typing, but Jake also contrived a sturdy desk out of one old packing case and a miniature chair out of another. Both articles of home-brewed furniture Jake insisted upon having painted before he permitted them inside his odd dwelling, and that delayed Jimmy one more day.

But it was only one more day; and then a new era of experience began for Jimmy.

It would be nice to report that he went at it with determination, self-discipline, and system, following instructions to the letter and emerging a first-rate typist.

Sorry. Jimmy hated every minute of it. He galled at the pages and pages of *juj juj juj frf frf frf*. He cried with frustration because he could not perform the simple exercise to perfection. He skipped through the book so close to complete failure that he hurled it across the room, and cried in anger because he had not the strength to throw the typewriter after it. Throw the machine? He had not the strength in his pinky to press the carriage-shift key!

Part of his difficulty was the size of his hands, of course. But most of his trouble lay deep-seated in his recollection of his parents' fabulous machine. It would have made a typist of him in a single half-hour session, or so he thought.

He had yet to learn about the vast gulf that lies between theory and practice.

It took Jimmy several weeks of aimless fiddling before he realized that there was no easy short-cut. Then he went back to the *juj juj juj frf frf frf* routine and hated it just as much, but went on.

He invented a kind of home-study "hooky" to break the monotony. He would run off a couple of pages of regular exercise, and then turn back to the hunt-and-peck system of typing to work on a story. He took a furtive glee in this; he felt that he was getting away with something. In mid-July, Jake caught him at it.

"What's going on?" demanded Jake, waving the pages of manuscript copy.

"Typing," said Jimmy.

Jake picked up the typing guidebook and waved it under Jimmy's nose. "Show me where it says you gotta type anything like, 'Captain Brandon struggled against his chains when he heard Lady Hamilton scream. The pirate's evil laugh rang through the ship. "Curse you—" ' "

Jake snorted.

"But—" said Jimmy faintly.

"But nothing!" snapped Jake. "Stop the drivel and learn that thing! You think I let you keep the machine just to play games? We gotta find a way to make it pay off. Learn it good!"

He stamped out, taking the manuscript with him. From that moment on, Jimmy's furtive career as an author went on only when Jake was either out for the evening or entertaining. In any case, he did not bother Jimmy further, evidently content to wait until Jimmy had "learned it good" before putting this new accomplishment to use. Nor did Jimmy bother him. It was a satisfactory arrangement for the time being. Jimmy hid his "work" under a pile of raw paper and completed it in late August. Then, with the brash assurance of youth, he packed and mailed his first finished manuscript to the editor of *Boy's Magazine*.

His typing progressed more satisfactorily than he realized, even though he was still running off page after page of repetitious exercise, leavened now and then by a page of idiotic sentences the letters of which were restricted to the center of the typewriter keyboard. The practice, even the hunt-and-peck relaxation from discipline, exercised the small muscles. Increased strength brought increased accuracy.

September rolled in, the streets emptied of school-aged children and the out-of-state car licenses diminished to a trickle. With the end of the carefree vacation days went the careless motorist.

Jake, whose motives were no more altruistic than his intentions were legal, began to look for a means of disposing of Jimmy Holden at the greatest profit to himself. Jake stalled only because he hoped that the reward might be stepped up.

But it was Jimmy's own operations that closed this chapter of his life.

CHAPTER FIVE

Jimmy had less scout work to do and no school to attend; he was too small to help in the sorting of car parts and too valuable to be tossed out. He was in the way.

So he was in Jake's office when the mail came. He brought the bundle to Jake's desk and sat on a box, sorting the circulars and catalogs from the first class. Halfway down the pile was a long envelope addressed to *Jimmy James.*

He dropped the rest with a little yelp. Jake eyed him quickly and snatched the letter out of Jimmy's hands.

"Hey! That's mine!" said Jimmy. Jake shoved him away.

"Who's writing you?" demanded Jake.

"It's mine!" cried Jimmy.

"Shut up!" snapped Jake, unfolding the letter. "I read *all* the mail that comes here first."

"But—"

"Shut your mouth and your teeth'll stay in," said Jake flatly. He separated a green slip from the letter and held the two covered while he read. "Well, well," he said. "Our little Shakespeare!" With a disdainful grunt Jake tossed the letter to Jimmy.

Eagerly, Jimmy took the letter and read:

Dear Mr. James:

We regret the unconscionable length of time between your submission and this reply. However, the fact that this reply is favorable may be its own apology. We are enclosing a check for $20.00 with the following explanation:

Our policy is to reject all work written in dialect. At the best we request the author to rewrite the piece in proper English and frame his effect by other means. Your little story is not dialect, nor is it bad literarily, the framework's being (as it is) a fairly good example of a small boy's relating in the first person one of his adventures, using for the first time his father's typewriter. But you went too far. I doubt that even a five-year-old would actually make as many typographical errors.

However, we found the idea amusing, therefore our payment. One of our editors will work your manuscript into less-erratic typescript for eventual publication.

Please continue to think of us in the future, but don't corn up your script with so many studied blunders.

Sincerely,
Joseph Brandon, editor,
Boy's Magazine.

"Gee," breathed Jimmy, "a check!"

Jake laughed roughly. "Shakespeare," he roared. "Don't corn up your stuff! You put too many errors in! Wow!"

Jimmy's eyes began to burn. He had no defense against this sarcasm. He wanted praise for having accomplished something, instead of raucous laughter.

"I wrote it," he said lamely.

"Oh, go away!" roared Jake.

Jimmy reached for the check.

"Scram," said Jake, shutting his laughter off instantly.

"It's mine!" cried Jimmy.

Jake paused, then laughed again. "Okay, smart kid. Take it and spend it!" He handed the check to Jimmy Holden.

Jimmy took it quickly and left.

He wanted to eye it happily, to gloat over it, to turn it over and over and to read it again and again; but he wanted to do it in private.

He took it with him to the nearest bank, feeling its folded bulk and running a fingernail along the serrated edge.

He re-read it in the bank, then went to a teller's window. "Can you cash this, please?" he asked.

The teller turned it over. "It isn't endorsed."

"I can't reach the desk to sign it," complained Jimmy.

"Have you an account here?" asked the teller politely.

"Well, no sir."

"Any identification?"

"No—no sir," said Jimmy thoughtfully. Not a shred of anything did he have to show who he was under either name.

"Who is this Jimmy James?" asked the teller.

"Me. I am."

The teller smiled. "And you wrote a short story that sold to *Boy's Magazine?*" he asked with a lifted eyebrow. "That's pretty good for a little guy like you."

"Yes sir."

The teller looked over Jimmy's head; Jimmy turned to look up at one of the bank's policemen. "Tom, what do you make of this?"

The policeman shrugged. He stooped down to Jimmy's level. "Where did you get this check, young fellow?" he asked gently.

"It came in the mail this morning."

"You're Jimmy James?"

"Yes sir." Jimmy Holden had been called that for more than half a year; his assent was automatic.

"How old are you, young man?" asked the policeman kindly.

"Five and a half."

"Isn't that a bit young to be writing stories?"

Jimmy bit his lip. "I wrote it, though."

The policeman looked up at the teller with a wink. "He can tell a good yarn," chuckled the policeman. "Shouldn't wonder if he could write one."

The teller laughed and Jimmy's eyes burned again. "It's mine," he insisted.

"If it's yours," said the policeman quietly, "we can settle it fast enough. Do your folks have an account here?"

"No sir."

"Hmmm. That makes it tough."

Brightly, Jimmy asked, "Can I open an account here?"

"Why, sure you can," said the policeman. "All you have to do is to bring your parents in."

"But I want the money," wailed Jimmy.

"Jimmy James," explained the policeman with a slight frown to the teller, "we can't cash a check without positive identification. Do you know what positive identification means?"

"Yes sir. It means that you've got to be sure that this is me."

"Right! Now, those are the rules. Now, of course, you don't look like the sort of young man who would tell a lie. I'll even bet your real name is Jimmy James, Jr. But you see, we have no proof, and our boss will be awful mad at us if we break the rules and cash this check without following the rules. The rules, Jimmy James, aren't to delay nice, honest people, but to stop people from making mistakes. Mistakes such as taking a little letter out of their father's mailbox. If we cashed that check, then it couldn't be put back in father's mailbox without anybody knowing about it. And that would be real bad."

"But it's mine!"

"Sonny, if that's yours, all you have to do is to have your folks come in and say so. Then we'll open an account for you."

"Yes sir," said Jimmy in a voice that was thick with tears of frustration close to the surface. He turned away and left.

Jake was still in the outside office of the Yard when Jimmy returned. The boy was crestfallen, frustrated, unhappy, and would not have returned at all if there had been another place where he was welcome. He expected ridicule from Jake, but Jake smiled.

"No luck, kid?"

Jimmy just shook his head.

"Checks are tough, Jimmy. Give up, now?"

"No!"

"No? What then?"

"I can write a letter and sign it," said Jimmy, explaining how he had outfoxed the ticket seller.

"Won't work with checks, Jimmy. For me now, if I was to be polite and dressed right they might cash a twenty if I showed up with my social security card, driver's license, identification card with photograph sealed in, and all that junk. But a kid hasn't got a chance. Look, Jimmy, I'm sorry for this morning. Tomorrow morning we'll go over to my bank and I'll have them cash it for you. It's yours. You earned it and you keep it. Okay? Are we friends again?"

"Yes sir."

Gravely they shook hands. "Watch the place, kid," said Jake. "I got to make a phone call."

In the morning, Jake dressed for business and insisted that Jimmy put on his best to make a good impression. After breakfast, they set out. Jake parked in front of a granite building.

"This isn't any bank," objected Jimmy. "This is a police station."

"Sure," responded Jake. "Here's where we get you an identification card. Don't you know?"

"Okay," said Jimmy dubiously.

Inside the station there were a number of men in uniform and in plain clothing. Jake strode forward, holding Jimmy by one small hand. They approached the sergeant's desk and Jake lifted Jimmy up and seated him on one edge of the desk with his feet dangling.

The sergeant looked at them with interest but without surprise.

"Sergeant," said Jake, "this is Jimmy James—as he calls himself when he's writing stories. Otherwise he is James Quincy Holden."

Jimmy went cold all over.

Jake backed through the circle that was closing in; the hole he made was filled by Paul Brennan.

It was not the first betrayal in Jimmy James's young life, but it was totally unexpected. He didn't know that the policeman from the bank had worried Jake; he didn't know that Jake had known all along who he was; he didn't know how fast Brennan had moved after the phone call from Jake. But his young mind leaped past the unknown facts to reach a certain, and correct, conclusion.

He had been sold out.

"Jimmy, Jimmy," came the old, pleading voice. "Why did you run away? Where have you been?"

Brennan stepped forward and placed a hand on the boy's shoulder. "Without a shadow of doubt," he said formally, "this is James Quincy Holden. I so identify him. And with no more ado, I hand you the reward." He reached into his inside pocket and drew out an envelope, handing it to Jake. "I have never parted with one thousand dollars so happily in my life."

Jimmy watched, unable to move. Brennan was busy and cheerful, the model of the man whose long-lost ward has been returned to him.

"So, James, shall we go quietly or shall we have a scene?"

Trapped and sullen, Jimmy Holden said nothing. The officers helped him down from the desk. He did not move. Brennan took him by a hand that was as limp as wet cloth. Brennan started for the door. The arm lifted until the link was taut; then, with slow, dragging steps, James Quincy Holden started toward home.

Brennan said, "You understand me, don't you, Jimmy?"

"You want my father's machine."

"Only to help you, Jimmy. Can't you believe that?"

"No."

Brennan drove his car with ease. A soft smile lurked around his lips. He went on, "You know what your father's machine will do for you, don't you, Jimmy?"

"Yes."

"But have you ever attended school?"

"No." But Jimmy remembered the long hours and hours of study and practice before he became proficient with his typewriter. For a moment he felt close to tears. It had been the only possession he truly owned, now it was gone. And with it was gone the author's first check. The thrill of that first check is far greater than Graduation or the First Job. It is approximately equal to the flush of pride that comes when the author's story hits print with his NAME appended.

But Jimmy's typewriter was gone, and his check was gone. Without a doubt the check would turn up cashed—through the operations of Jake Caslow.

Brennán's voice cut into his thoughts. "You will attend school, Jimmy. You'll have to."

"But—"

"Oh, now look, Jimmy. There are laws that say you must attend school. The only way those laws can be avoided is to make an appeal to the law itself, and have your legal guardian—myself—ask for the privilege of tutoring you at home. Well, I won't do it."

He drove for a moment, thinking. "So you're going to attend school," he said, "and while you're there you're going to be careful not to disclose by any act or inference that you already know everything they can teach you. Otherwise they will ask some embarrassing questions. And the first thing that happens to you is that you will be put in a much harder place to escape from than our home, Jimmy. Do you understand?"

"Yes sir," the boy said sickly.

"But," purred Uncle Paul Brennan, "you may find school very boring. If so, you have only to say the word—rebuild your father's machine—and go on with your career."

"I w—" Jimmy began automatically, but his uncle stopped him.

"You won't, no," he agreed. "Not now. In the meantime, then, you will live the life proper to your station—and your age. I won't deny you a single thing, Jimmy. Not a single thing that a five-year-old can want."

CHAPTER SIX

Paul Brennan moved into the Holden house with Jimmy.

Jimmy had the run of the house—almost. Uncle Paul closed off the upper sitting room, which the late parents had converted into their laboratory. *That* was locked. But the rest of the house was free, and Jimmy was once more among the things he had never hoped to see again.

Brennan's next step was to hire a middle-aged couple to take care of house and boy. Their name was Mitchell; they were childless and regretted it; they lavished on Jimmy the special love and care that comes only from childless child-lovers.

Though Jimmy was wary to the point of paranoia, he discovered that he wanted for nothing. He was kept clean and his home kept tidy. He was fed well—not only in terms of nourishment, but in terms of what he liked.

Then . . . Jimmy begin to notice changes.

Huckleberry Finn turned up missing. In its place on the shelf was a collection of Little Golden Books.

His advanced Mecanno set was "broken"—so Mrs. Mitchell told him. Uncle Paul had accidentally crushed it. "But you'll like this better," she beamed, handing him a fresh new box from the toy store. It contained bright-colored modular blocks.

Jimmy's parents had given him canvasboard and oil paints; now they were gone. Jimmy would have admitted he was no artist; but he didn't enjoy retrogressing to his uncle's selection—finger paints.

His supply of drawing paper was not tampered with. But it was not replaced. When it was gone, Jimmy was presented with a blackboard and boxes of colored chalk.

By Christmas every possession was gone—replaced—the new toys tailored to Jimmy's physical age. There was a Christmas tree, and under it a pile of gay bright boxes. Jimmy had hardly the heart to open them, for he knew what they would contain.

He was right.

Jimmy had everything that would keep a five-year-old boy contented . . . and not one iota more. He objected; his objections got him nowhere. Mrs. Mitchell was reproachful: Ingratitude, Jimmy! Mr. Mitchell was scornful: Maybe James would like to vote and smoke a pipe?

And Paul Brennan was very clear. There was a way out of this, yes. Jimmy could have whatever he liked. There was just this one step that must be taken first; the machine must be put back together again.

When it came time for Jimmy to start school he was absolutely delighted; nothing, nothing could be worse than this.

At first it was a novel experience.

He sat at a desk along with forty-seven other children of his size, neatly stacked in six aisles with eight desks to the tier. He did his best to copy their manners and to reproduce their halting speech and imperfect grammar. For the first couple of weeks he was not noticed.

The teacher, with forty-eight young new minds to study, gave him his 2.08% of her total time and attention. Jimmy Holden was not a deportment problem; his answers to the few questions she directed at him were correct. Therefore he needed less attention and got less; she spent her time on the loud, the unruly and those who lagged behind in education.

Because his total acquaintance with children of his own age had been among the slum kids that hung around Jake Caslow's Place, Jimmy found his new companions an interesting bunch.

He watched them, and he listened to them. He copied them and in two weeks Jimmy found them pitifully lacking and hopelessly misinformed. They could not remember at noon what they had been told at ten o'clock. They had difficulty in reading the simple pages of the First Reader.

But he swallowed his pride and stumbled on and on, mimicking his friends and remaining generally unnoticed.

If written examinations were the rule in the First Grade, Jimmy would have been discovered on the first one. But with less than that 2% of the teacher's time directed at him, Jimmy's run of correct answers did not attract notice. His boredom and his lack of attention during daydreams made him seem quite normal.

He began to keep score on his classmates on the flyleaf of one of his books. Jimmy was a far harsher judge than the teacher. He marked them either wrong or right; he gave no credit for trying, or for their stumbling efforts to express their muddled ideas and incomplete grasp. He found their games fun at first, but quickly grew bored. When he tried to introduce a note of strategy they ignored him because they did not understand. They made rules as they went along and changed them as they saw fit. Then, instead of complying with their own rules, they pouted-up and sulked when they couldn't do as they wanted.

But in the end it was Jimmy's lack of experience in acting that tripped him.

Having kept score on his playmates' answers, Jimmy knew that some fairly high percentage of answers must inevitably be wrong. So he embarked upon a program of supplying a certain proportion of errors. He discovered that supplying a wrong answer that was consistent with the age of his contemporaries took too much of his intellect to keep his actions straight. He forgot to employ halting speech and childlike grammar. His errors were delivered in faultless grammar and excellent self-expression; his correct answers came out in the English of his companions; mispronounced, ill-composed, and badly delivered.

The contrast was enough to attract even 2.08% of a teacher.

During the third week of school, Jimmy was daydreaming during class. Abruptly his teacher snapped, "James Holden, how much is seven times nine?"

"Sixty-three," replied Jimmy, completely automatic.

"James," she said softly, "do you know the rest of your numbers?'

Jimmy looked around like a trapped animal. His teacher waited him out until Jimmy, finding no escape, said, "Yes'm."

"Well," she said with a bright smile. "It's nice to know that you do. Can you do the multiplication table?"

"Yes'm."

"Are you sure?"

"Yes'm."

"Let's hear you."

Jimmy looked around. "No, Jimmy," said his teacher. "I want you to say it. Go ahead." And then as Jimmy hesitated still, she addressed the class. "This is important," she said. "Someday you will have to learn it, too. You will use it all through life and the earlier you learn it the better off you all will be. *Knowledge,*" she quoted proudly, *"is power!* Now, Jimmy!"

Jimmy began with two-times-two and worked his way through the long table to the twelves. When he finished, his teacher appointed one of the better-behaved children to watch the class. "Jimmy," she said, "I'm going to see if we can't put you up in the next grade. You don't belong here. Come along."

They went to the principal's office. "Mr. Whitworth," said Jimmy's teacher, "I have a young genius in my class."

"A young genius, Miss Tilden?"

"Yes, indeed. He already knows the multiplication table."

"You do, James? Where did you learn it?"

"My father taught me."

Principal and teacher looked at each another. They said nothing but they were both recalling stories and rumors about the brilliance of his parents. The accident and death had not escaped notice.

"What else did they teach you, James?" asked Mr. Whitworth. "To read and write, of course?"

"Yes sir."

"History?"

Jimmy squirmed inwardly. He did not know how much to admit. "Some," he said noncommittally.

"When did Columbus discover America?"

"In Fourteen Ninety-Two."

"Fine," said Mr. Whitworth with a broad smile. He looked at Miss Tilden. "You're right. Young James should be advanced." He looked down at Jimmy Holden. "James," he said, "we're going to place you in the Second Grade for a tryout. Unless we're wrong, you'll stay and go up with them."

Jimmy's entry into Second Grade brought a different attitude. He had entered school quietly just for the sake of getting away from Paul Brennan. Now he was beginning to form a plan. If he could go from First to Second in a matter of three weeks, then, by carefully disclosing his store of knowledge bit-by-bit at the proper moment, he might be able to go through school in a short time. Moreover, he had tasted the first fruits of recognition. He craved more.

Somewhere was born the quaint notion that getting through school would automatically make him an adult, with all attendant privileges.

So Jimmy Holden dropped all pretense. His answers were as right as he could make them. He dropped the covering mimickry of childish speech and took personal pride in using grammar as good as that of his teacher.

This got him nothing. The Second Grade teacher was of the "progressive" school; she firmly believed that everybody, having been created equal, had to stay that way. She pointedly avoided giving Jimmy any opportunity to show his capability.

He bided his time with little grace.

He found his opportunity during the visit of a school superintendent. During this session Jimmy hooted when one of his fellows said that Columbus proved the world was round.

Angrily she demanded that Jimmy tell her who did prove it, and Jimmy Holden replied that he didn't know whether it was Pythagoras or one of his followers, but he did know that it was one of the few things that Aristotle ever got right. This touched her on a sore spot. She admired Aristotle and couldn't bear to hear the great man accused of error.

She started baiting Jimmy with loaded questions and stopped when Jimmy stated that Napoleon Bonaparte was responsible for the invention of canned food, the adoption of the metric system, and the development of the semaphore telegraph. This stopped all proceedings until Jimmy himself found the references in the Britannica. That little feat of research-reference impressed the visiting superintendent. Jimmy Holden was jumped into Third Grade.

Convinced that he was on the right trolley, Jimmy proceeded to plunge in with both feet. Third Grade Teacher helped. Within a week he was being called upon to aid the laggards. He stood out like a lighthouse; he was the one who could supply the right answers when the class was stumped. His teacher soon began to take a delight in belaboring the class for a minute before turning to Jimmy for the answer. Heaven forgive him, Jimmy enjoyed it.

He began to hold back slyly, like a comedian building up the tension before a punch-line.

His classmates began to call him "old know-it-all." Jimmy did not realize that it was their resentment speaking. He accepted it as deference to his superior knowledge. The fact that he was not a part of their playtime life did not bother him one iota. He knew very well that his size alone would cut him out of the rough and heavy games of his classmates; he did not know that he was cut out of their games because they disliked him.

As time wore on, some of the rougher ones changed his nickname from "know-it-all" to "teacher's pet"; one of them used rougher language still. To this Jimmy replied in terms he'd learned from Jake Caslow's gutters. All that saved him from a beating was his size; even the ones who disliked him would not stand for the bully's beating up a smaller child.

But in other ways they picked on him. Jimmy reasoned out his own relationship between intelligence and violence. He had yet to learn the psychology of vandalism—but he was experiencing it.

Finding no enjoyment out of play periods, Jimmy took to staying in. The permissive school encouraged it; if Jimmy Holden preferred to tinker with a typewriter instead of playing noisy games, his teacher saw no wrong in it—for his Third Grade teacher was something of an intellectual herself.

In April, one week after his sixth birthday, Jimmy Holden was jumped again.

Jimmy entered Fourth Grade to find that his fame had gone before him; he was received with sullen glances and turned backs.

But he did not care. For his birthday, he received a typewriter from Paul Brennan. Brennan never found out that the note suggesting it from Jimmy's Third Grade teacher had been written after Jimmy's prompting.

So while other children played, Jimmy wrote.

He was not immediately successful. His first several stories were returned; but eventually he drew a winner and a check. Armed with superior knowledge, Jimmy mailed it to a bank that was strong in advertising "mail-order" banking. With his first check he opened a pay-by-the-item, no-minimum-balance checking account.

Gradually his batting average went up, but there were enough returned rejections to make Paul Brennan view Jimmy's literary effort with quiet amusement. Still, slowly and in secret, Jimmy built up his bank balance by twenties, fifties, an occasional hundred.

For above everything, by now Jimmy knew that he could not go on through school as he'd planned.

If his entry into Fourth Grade had been against scowls and resentment from his classmates, Fifth and Sixth would be more so. Eventually the day would come when he would be held back. He was already mingling with children far beyond his size. The same permissive school that graduated dolts so that their stupid personalities wouldn't be warped would keep him back by virtue of the same idiotic reasoning.

He laid his plans well. He covered his absence from school one morning and thereby gained six free hours to start going about his own business before his absence could be noticed.

This was his third escape. He prayed that it would be permanent.

BOOK TWO:
THE HERMIT

CHAPTER SEVEN

Seventy-five miles south of Chicago there is a whistle-stop called Shipmont. (No ship has ever been anywhere near it; neither has a mountain.) It lives because of a small college; the college, in turn, owes its maintenance to an installation of great interest to the Atomic Energy Commission.

Shipmont is served by two trains a day—which stop only when there is a passenger to get on or off, which isn't often. These passengers, generally speaking, are oddballs carrying attaché cases or eager young men carrying minature slide rules.

But on this day came a woman and a little girl.

Their total visible possessions were two battered suitcases and one battered trunk. The little girl was neatly dressed, in often-washed and mended clothing; she carried a small covered basket, and there were breadcrumbs visible on the lid. She looked bewildered, shy and frightened. She was.

The mother was thirty, though there were lines of worry on her forehead and around her eyes that made her look older. She wore little makeup and her clothing had been bought for wear instead of for looks. She looked around, leaned absently down to pat the little girl and straightened as the station-master came slowly out.

"Need anything, ma'am?" He was pleasant enough. Janet Bagley appreciated that; life had not been entirely pleasant for her for some years.

"I need a taxicab, if there is one."

"There is. I run it after the train gets in for them as ain't met. You're not goin' to the college?" He pronounced it "collitch."

Janet Bagley shook her head and took a piece of paper from her bag. "Mr. Charles Maxwell, Rural Route Fifty-three, Martin's Hill Road," she read. Her daughter began to whimper.

The station-master frowned. "Hum," he said, "that's the Herm—er, d'you know him?"

Mrs. Bagley said: "I've never met him. What kind of a man is he?"

That was the sort of question the station-master appreciated. His job was neither demanding nor exciting; an opportunity to talk was worth having. He said cheerfully, "Why, I don't rightly know, ma'am. Nobody's ever seen him."

"Nobody?"

"Nope. Nobody. Does everything by mail."

"My goodness, what's the matter with him?"

"Don't rightly know, ma'am. Story is he was once a professor and got in some kind of big explosion. Burned the hide off'n his face and scarred up his hands something turrible, so he don't want to show himself. Rented the house by mail, pays his rent by mail. Orders stuff by mail. Mostly not real U-nited States Mail, y'know, because we don't mind dropping off a note to someone in town. I'm the local mailman, too. So when I find a note to Herby Wharton, the fellow that owns the general store, I drop it off. Margie Clark over at the bank says he writes. Gets checks from New York from publishing companies." The station-master looked around as if he were looking for Soviet spies. "He's a scientist, all right. He's doin' something important and hush-hush up there. Lots and lots of boxes and packin' cases I've delivered up there from places like Central Scientific and Labo—tory Supply Company. Must be a smart feller. You visitin' him?"

"Well, he hired me for housekeeper. By mail." Mrs. Bagley looked puzzled and concerned.

Little Martha began to cry.

"It'll be all right," said the station-master soothingly. "You keep your eye open," he said to Mrs. Bagley. "Iff'n you see anything out of line, you come right back and me and the missus will give you a lift. But he's all right. Nothin' goin' on up there that I know of. Fred Riordan—he's the sheriff—has watched the place for days and days and it's always quiet. No visitors. No nothin'. Know what I think? I think he's experimenting with something to take away the burn scars. That's whut I think. Well, hop in and I'll drive you out there."

"Is it going to cost much?"

"Nothin' this trip. We'll charge it to the U-nited States Mail. Got a package goin' out. Was waitin' for something else to go along with it, but you're here and we can count that. This way to the only taxicab service in Shipmont."

The place looked deserted. It was a shabby old clapboard house; the architecture of the prosperous farmer of seventy-five years ago. The grounds were spacious but the space was filled with scrub weeds. A picket fence surrounded the weeds with uncertain security. The windows—those that could be seen, that is—were dirty enough to prevent seeing inside with clarity, and what transparency there was left was covered by curtains. The walk up the "lawn" was flagstone with crabgrass between the stones.

The station-master unshipped the small trunk and stood it just inside the fence. He parked the suitcases beside it. "Never go any farther than this," he explained. "So far's I know, you're the first person to ever head up thet walk to the front door."

Mrs. Bagley rapped on the door. It opened almost instantly.

"I'm—" then Mrs. Bagley dropped her eyes to the proper level. To the lad who was standing there she said, "I'm Mrs. Bagley. Your father—a Mr. Charles Maxwell is expecting me."

"Come in," said Jimmy Holden. "Mr. Maxwell— well, he isn't my father. He sent me to let you in."

Mrs. Bagley entered and dropped her suitcases in the front hall. Martha held back behind her mother's skirt. Jimmy closed the door and locked it carefully, but left the key in the keyhole with a gesture that Mrs. Bagley could not mistake. "Please come in here and sit down," said James Holden. "Relax a moment." He turned to look at the girl. He smiled at her, but she cowered behind her mother's skirt as if she wanted to bury her face but was afraid to lose sight of what was going on around her.

"What's your name?" asked James.

She retreated, hiding most of her face. Mrs. Bagley stroked her hair and said, "Now, Martha, come on. Tell the little boy your name."

Purely as a matter of personal pride, James Holden objected to the "little boy" but he kept his peace because he knew that at eight years old he was still a little boy. In a soothing way, James said, "Come on out, Martha. I'll show you some girl-type toys we've got."

The girl's head emerged slowly, "I'm Martha Bagley," she announced.

"How old are you?"

"I'm seven."

"I'm eight," stated James. "Come on."

Mrs. Bagley looked around. She saw that the dirt on the windows was all on the outside. The inside was clean. So was the room. So were the curtains. The room needed a dusting—a most thorough dusting. It had been given a haphazard lick-and-a-promise cleanup not too long ago, but the cleanup before that had been as desultory as the last, and without a doubt the one before and the one before that had been of the same sort of half-hearted cleaning. As a woman and a housekeeper, Mrs. Bagley found the room a bit strange.

The furniture caught her eye first. A standard open bookcase, a low sofa, a very low cocktail-type table. The chair she stood beside was standard looking, so was the big easy chair opposite. Yet she felt large in the room despite its old-fashioned high ceiling. There were several low footstools in the room; ungraceful things that were obviously wooden boxes covered with padding and leatherette. The straight chair beside her had been lowered; the bottom rung between the legs was almost on the floor.

She realized why she felt big. The furniture in the room had all been cut down.

She continued to look. The strangeness continued to bother her and she realized that there were no ash trays; there was none of the usual clutter of things that a family drops in their tracks. It was a room fashioned for a small person to live in but it wasn't lived-in.

The lack of hard cleanliness did not bother her very much. There had been an effort here, and the fact that this Charles Maxwell was hiring a housekeeper was in itself a statement that the gentleman knew that he needed one. It was odd, but it wasn't ominous.

She shook her daughter gently and said, "Come on, Martha. Let's take a look at these girl-type toys."

James led them through a short hallway, turned left at the first door, and then stood aside to give them a full view of the room. It was a playroom for a girl. It was cleaner than the living room, and as—well, untouched. It had been furnished with girl-toys that some catalog "recommended as suitable for a girl of seven."

The profusion of toys overwhelmed little Martha. She stood just inside of the door with her eyes wide, glancing back and forth. She took one slow step forward, then another. Then she quickened. She moved through the room looking, then putting out a slow, hesitant hand to touch very gently. Tense, as if she were waiting for the warning not to touch, Martha finally caressed the hair of a baby doll.

Mrs. Bagley smiled. "I'll have a time prying her loose from here," she said.

James nodded his head. "Let her amuse herself for a bit," he said. "With Martha occupied, you can give your attention to a more delicate matter."

Mrs. Bagley forgot that she was addressing an eight-year-old boy. His manner and his speech bemused her. "Yes," she said. "I do want to get this settled with your mysterious Charles Maxwell. Do you expect him down, or shall I go upstairs—?"

"This may come as a shock, Mrs. Bagley, but Charles Maxwell isn't here."

"Isn't here?" she echoed, in a tone of voice that clearly indicated that she had heard the words but hadn't really grasped their full meaning. "He won't be gone long, will he?"

James watched her covertly, then said in a matter-of-fact voice, "He left you a letter."

"Letter?"

"He was called away on some urgent business."

"But—"

"Please read the letter. It explains everything."

He handed her an envelope addressed to "Mrs. Janet Bagley." She looked at it from both sides, in the womanlike process of trying to divine its contents instead of opening it. She looked at James, but James sat stolidly waiting. Mrs. Bagley was going to get no more information from him until she read that letter, and James was prepared to sit it out until she did. It placed Mrs. Bagley in the awkward position of having to decide what to do next. Then the muffled sound of little-girl crooning came from the distant room. That brought the realization that as odd as this household was, it was a *home*. Mrs. Bagley delayed no further. She opened the letter and read:

My Dear Mrs. Bagley:

I deeply regret that I am not there to greet you, but it was not possible. However, please understand that insofar as I am concerned, you were hired and have been drawing your salary from the date that I forwarded railroad fare and traveling expenses. Any face-to-face meeting is no more than a pleasantry, a formal introduction. It must not be considered in any way connected with the thought of a "Final Interview" or the process of "Closing the Deal."

Please carry on as if you had been in charge long before I departed, or—considering my hermitlike habits—the way you would have carried on if I had not departed, but instead was still upstairs and hard at work with most definite orders that I was not to be disturbed for anything less important than total, personal disaster.

I can offer you a word of explanation about young James. You will find him extraordinarily competent for a youngster of eight years. Were he less competent, I might have delayed my departure long enough to pass him literally from my supervision to yours. However, James is quite capable of taking care of himself; this fact you will appreciate fully long before you and I meet face-to-face.

In the meantime, remember that our letters and the other references acquaint us with one another far better than a few short hours of personal contact.

Sincerely,
Charles Maxwell

"Well!" said Mrs. Bagley. "I don't know what to say."

Jimmy smiled. "You don't have to say anything," he said.

Mrs. Bagley looked at the youngster. "I don't think I like your Mr. Maxwell," she said.

"Why not?"

"He's practically shanghaied me here. He knows very well that I couldn't possibly leave you here all alone, no matter how I disliked the situation. He's practically forced me to stay."

James suppressed a smile. He said, "Mrs. Bagley, the way the trains run in and out of Shipmont, you're stuck for an overnight stay in any case."

"You don't seem to be perturbed."

"I'm not," he said.

Mrs. Bagley looked at James carefully. His size; his physique was precisely that of the eight-year-old boy. There was nothing malformed nor out-of-proportion; yet he spoke with an adult air of confidence.

"I am," she admitted.

"Perturbed? You needn't be," he said. "You've got to remember that writers are an odd lot. They don't conform. They don't punch time-clocks. They boast of having written a novel in three weeks but they don't mention the fact that they sat around drinking beer for six months plotting it."

"Meaning what?"

"Meaning that Maxwell sees nothing wrong in attending to his own affairs and expecting you to attend to yours."

"But what shall I do?"

James smiled. "First, take a look around the house and satisfy yourself. You'll find the third floor shut off; the rooms up there are Maxwell's, and no one goes in but him. My bedroom is the big one in the front of the second floor. Pick yourself a room or a suite of rooms or move in all over the rest of the house. Build yourself a cup of tea and relax. Do as he says: Act as if you'd arrived before he took off, that you'd met and agreed verbally to do what you've already agreed to do by letter. Look at it from his point of view."

"What is his point of view?"

"He's a writer. He rented this house by mail. He banks by mail and shops by mail and makes his living by writing. Don't be surprised when he hires a housekeeper by mail and hands her the responsibility in writing. He lives by the written word."

Mrs. Bagley said, "In other words, the fact that he offered me a job in writing and I took it in writing—?"

"Writing," said James Holden soberly, "was invented for the express purpose of recording an agreement between two men in a permanent form that could be read by other men. The whole world runs on the theory that no one turns a hand until names are signed to written contracts—and here you sit, not happy because you weren't contracted-for by a personal chit-chat and a handshake."

Mrs. Bagley was taken aback slightly by this rather pointed criticism. What hurt was the fact that, generally speaking, it was true and especially the way he put it. The young man was too blunt, too outspokenly direct. Obviously he needed someone around the place who wasn't the self-centered writer-type. And, Mrs. Bagley admitted to herself, there certainly was no evidence of evil-doing here.

No matter what, Charles Maxwell had neatly trapped her into staying by turning her own maternal responsibility against her.

"I'll get my bags," she said.

James Holden took a deep breath. He'd won this hurdle, so far so good. Now for the next!

Mrs. Bagley found life rather unhurried in the days that followed. She relaxed and tried to evaluate James Holden. To her unwarned mind, the boy was quite a puzzle.

There was no doubt about his eight years, except that he did not whoop and holler with the aimlessness of the standard eight-year-old boy. His vocabulary was far ahead of the eight-year-old and his speech was in adult grammar rather than halting. It was, she supposed, due to his constant adult company; children denied their contemporaries for playmates often take on attitudes beyond their years. Still, it was a bit on the too-superior side to please her. It was as if he were the result of over-indulgent parents who'd committed the mistake of letting the child know that their whole universe revolved about him.

Yet Maxwell's letters said that he was motherless, that he was not Maxwell's son. This indicated a probable history of broken homes and remarriages. Mrs. Bagley thought the problem over and gave it up. It was a home.

Things went on. They started warily but smoothly at first with Mrs. Bagley asking almost incessantly whether Mr. Maxwell would approve of this or that and should she do this or the other and, phrased cleverly, indicated that she would take the word of young James for the time being but there would be evil sputterings in the fireplace if the programs approved by young James Holden were not wholly endorsed by Mr. Charles Maxwell.

At the end of the first week, supplies were beginning to run short and still there was no sign of any return of the missing Mr. Maxwell. With some misgiving, Mrs. Bagley broached the subject of shopping to James. The youngster favored Mrs. Bagley with another smile.

"Yes," he said calmly. "Just a minute." And he disappeared upstairs to fetch another envelope. Inside was a second letter which read:

My Dear Mrs. Bagley:
    Attached you will find letters addressed to several of the local merchants in Shipmont, explaining your status as my housekeeper and directing them to honor your purchases against my accounts. Believe me, they recognize my signature despite the fact that they might not recognize me! There should be no difficulty. I'd

suggest, however, that you start a savings account at the local bank with the enclosed salary check. You have no idea how much weight the local banker carries in his character-reference of folks with a savings account.

Otherwise, I trust things are pleasant.

Sincerely,
Charles Maxwell.

"Things," she mused aloud, "are pleasant enough."

James nodded. "Good," he said. "You're satisfied, then?"

Mrs. Bagley smiled at him wistfully. "As they go," she said, "I'm satisfied. Lord knows, you're no great bother, James, and I'll be most happy to tell Mr. Maxwell so when he returns."

James nodded. "You're not concerned over Maxwell, are you?"

She sobered. "Yes," she said in a whisper. "Yes, I am. I'm afraid that he'll change things, that he'll not approve of Martha, or the way dinner is made, or my habits in dishwashing or bedmaking or marketing or something that will—well, put me right in the role of a paid chambermaid, a servant, a menial with no more to say about the running of the house, once he returns."

James Holden hesitated, thought, then smiled.

"Mrs. Bagley," he said apologetically, "I've thrown you a lot of curves. I hope you won't mind one more."

The woman frowned. James said hurriedly, "Oh, it's nothing bad, believe me. I mean—Well, you'll have to judge for yourself.

"You see, Mrs. Bagley," he said earnestly, "there isn't any Charles Maxwell."

Janet Bagley, with the look of a stricken animal, sat down heavily. There were two thoughts suddenly in her mind: *Now I've got to leave,* and, *But I can't leave.*

She sat looking at the boy, trying to make sense of what he had said. Mrs. Bagley was a young woman, but she had lived a demanding and unrelenting life; her husband dead, her finances calamitous, a baby to feed and raise . . . there had been enough trouble in her life and she sought no more.

But she was also a woman of some strength of character.

Janet Bagley had not been able to afford much joy, but when things were at their worst she had not wept. She had been calm. She had taken what inexpensive pleasures she could secure—the health of her daughter, the strength of her arms to earn a living, the cunning of her mind to make a dollar do the work of five. She had learned that there was no bargain that was not worth investigating; the shoddiest goods were worth owning at a price; the least attractive prospect had to be faced and understood, for any commodity becomes a bargain when the price is right. There was no room for laziness or indulgence in her life. There was also no room for panic.

So Janet Bagley thought for a moment, and then said: "Tell me what you're talking about, James."

James Holden said immediately: "I am Charles Maxwell. That is, 'Charles Maxwell' is a pen name. He has no other existence."

"But—"

"But it's true, Mrs. Bagley," the boy said earnestly. "I'm only eight years old, but I happen to be earning my own living—as a writer, under the name of, among others, Charles Maxwell. Perhaps you've looked up some of the 'Charles Maxwell' books? If so, you may have seen some of the book reviews that were quoted on the jackets—I remember one that said that Charles Maxwell writes as though he himself were a boy, with the education of an adult. Well, that's the fact of the case."

Mrs. Bagley said slowly, "But I did look Mr. Max—
I mean, I did look you up. There was a complete bio-
graphical sketch in *Woman's Life*. Thirty-one years
old, I remember."

"I know. I wrote it. It too was fiction."

"You wrote—but why?"

"Because I was asked to write it," said James.

"But, well—what I mean, is—Just who is Mr.
Maxwell? The man at the station said something
about a hermit, but—"

"The Hermit of Martin's Hill is a convenient character carefully prepared to explain what might have
looked like a very odd household," said James
Holden. "Charles Maxwell, the Hermit, does not exist
except in the minds of the neighbors and the editors
of several magazines, and of course, the readers of
those pages."

"But he wrote me himself." The bewildered
woman paused.

"That's right, Mrs. Bagley. There's absolutely nothing illegal about a writer's using a pen name. Absolutely nothing. Some writers become so well-known by
their pseudonym that they answer when someone
calls them. So long as the writer isn't wanted by the
F.B.I. for some heinous crime, and so long as he can
unscramble the gobbledygook on Form 1040, stay out
of trouble, pay his rent, and make his regular con-
tributions to Social Security, nobody cares what name
he uses."

"But where are your parents? Have you no friends?
No legal guardian? Who handles your business affairs?"

James said in a flat tone of recital, "My parents are
dead. What friends and family I have, want to turn
me over to my legal guardian. My legal guardian is
the murderer of my parents and the would-have-been
murderer of me if I hadn't been lucky. Someday I
shall prove it. And I handle my affairs myself, by

mail, as you well know. I placed the advertisement, wrote the letters of reply, wrote those letters that answered specific questions and asked others, and I wrote the check that you cashed in order to buy your railroad ticket, Mrs. Bagley. No, don't worry. It's good."

Mrs. Bagley tried to digest all that and failed. She returned to the central point. "But you're a minor—"

"I am," admitted James Holden. "But you accepted my checks, your bank accepted my checks, and they've been honored by the clearing houses. My own bank has been accepting them for a couple of years now. It will continue to be that way until something goes wrong and I'm found out. I'm taking every precaution that nothing goes wrong."

"Still—"

"Mrs. Bagley, look at me. I am precisely what I seem to be. I am a young male human being, eight years old, possessed of a good command of the English language and an education superior to the schooling of any high-school graduate. It is true that I am an infant in the eyes of the law, so I have not the right to hold the ear of the law long enough to explain my competence."

"But—"

"Listen a moment," insisted James. "You can't hope to hear it all in one short afternoon. It may take weeks before you fully understand."

"You assume that I'll stay, then?"

James smiled. Not the wide open, simple smile of youth but the knowing smile of someone pleased with the success of his own plans. "Mrs. Bagley, of the many replies to my advertisement, yours was selected because you are in a near-desperate position. My advertisement must have sounded tailor-made to fit your case; a young widow to work as resident housekeeper, child of preschool or early school age welcome. Well, Mrs. Bagley, your qualifications are tailor-made for me, too. You are in need, and I can give you what you need—a living salary, a home for you and your daughter, and for your daughter an education that will far transcend any that you could ever provide for her."

"And how do you intend to make that come to pass?"

"Mrs. Bagley, at the present time there are only two people alive who know the answer to that question. I am one of them. The other is my so-called legal 'guardian' who would be most happy to guard me right out of my real secret. You will be the third person alive to know that my mother and father built a machine that produces the same deeply-inlaid memory-track of information as many months of learning-by-repetition. With that machine, I absorbed the information available to a high-school student before I was five. I am rebuilding that machine now from plans and specifications drilled into my brain by my father. When it is complete, I intend to become the best informed person in the world."

"That isn't right," breathed Mrs. Bagley.

"Isn't it?" asked James seriously. "Isn't it right? Is it wrong, when at the present time it takes a man until he is almost thirty years old before he can say that his education is complete?"

"Well, I suppose you're right."

James eyed Mrs. Bagley carefully. He said softly, "Mrs. Bagley, tell me, would you give Martha a college education if you had—or will you if you have at the time—the wherewithal to provide it?"

"Of course."

"You have it here," said James. "So long as you stay to protect it."

"But won't it make—?" her voice trailed away uncertainly.

"A little intellectual monster out of her?" laughed the boy. "Maybe. Maybe I am, too. On the other hand it might make a brilliant woman out of her. She might be a doctor if she has the capacity of a brilliant doctor. My father's machine is no monster-maker, Mrs. Bagley. With it a person could memorize the Britannica. And from the Britannica that person would learn that there is much good in the world and also that there is rich reward for being a part of that capacity for good."

"I seem to have been outmaneuvered," said Mrs. Bagley with a worried frown.

James smiled. "Not at all," he said. "It was just a matter of finding someone who wanted desperately to have what I wanted to give, and of course overcoming the natural adult reluctance to admit that anybody my size and age can operate on grown-up terms."

"You sound so sure of yourself."

"I am sure of myself. And one of the more important things in life is to understand one's limitations."

"But couldn't you convince them—?"

"One—you—I can convince. Maybe another, later. But if I tackle the great American public, I'm licked by statistics. My guess is that there is one brand-new United States citizen born every ten seconds. It takes me longer than ten seconds to convince someone that I know what I'm talking about. But so long as I have an accepted adult out front, running the store, I don't have to do anything but sit backstage, run the hidden strings, and wait until my period of growth provides me with a stature that won't demand any explanation."

From the playroom, Martha came running. "Mummy! Mummy!" she cried in a shrill voice filled with the strident tones of alarm, "Dolly's sick and I can't leave her!"

Mrs. Bagley folded her daughter in her arms. "We won't leave," she said. "We're staying."

James Holden nodded with satisfaction, but one

thing he realized then and there: He simply had to rush the completion of his father's machine.

He could not stand the simpering prattle of Martha Bagley's playgames.

CHAPTER EIGHT

The arrival of Mrs. Bagley changed James Holden's way of life far more than he'd expected. His basic idea had been to free himself from the hours of dishwashing, bedmaking, dusting, cleaning and straightening and from the irking chore of planning his meals far enough ahead to obtain sustenance either through mail or carried note. He gave up his haphazard chores readily. Mrs. Bagley's menus often served him dishes that he wouldn't have given house-room; but he also enjoyed many meals that he could not or would not have taken the time to prepare.

He did have some faint notion that being freed from the household toil would allow him sixteen or eighteen hours at the typewriter, but he was not greatly dismayed to find that this did not work.

When he wrote himself out, he relaxed by reading, or sitting quietly planning his next piece. Even that did not fill his entire day. To take some advantage of his time, James began to indulge in talk-fests with Mrs. Bagley.

These were informative. He was learning from her how the outside world was run, from one who had no close association with his own former life. Mrs. Bagley was by no means well-informed on all sides of life, but she did have her opinions and her experiences and a fair idea of how things went on in her own level. And, of course, James had made this choice because of the girl. He wanted a companion of his own age. Regardless of what Mrs. Bagley really thought of this matter of rapid education, James proposed to use it on Martha. That would give him a companion of his own like, they would come closer to understanding one another than he could ever hope to find understanding elsewhere.

So he talked and played with Martha in his moments of relaxation. And he found her grasp of life completely unreal.

James could not get through to her. He could not make her stop play-acting in everything that she did not ignore completely. It worried him.

With the arrival of summer, James and Martha played outside in the fresh air. They made a few shopping excursions into town, walking the mile and more by taking their time, and returning with their shopping load in the station-master's taxicab mail car. But on these expeditions, James hung close to Martha lest her babbling prattle start an unwelcome line of thought. She never did it, but James was forever on edge.

This source of possible danger drove him hard. The machine that was growing in a mare's-nest on the second floor began to evolve faster.

James Holden's work was a strangely crude efficiency. The prototype had been built by his father bit by bit and step by step as its design demanded. Sections were added as needed, and other sections believed needed were abandoned as the research showed them unnecessary. Louis Holden had been a fine instrumentation engineer, but his first models were haywired in the breadboard form. James copied his father's work—including his father's casual breadboard style. And he added some inefficiencies of his own.

Furthermore, James was not strong enough to lift the heavier assemblies into place. James parked the parts wherever they would sit.

To Mrs. Bagley, the whole thing was bizarre and unreasonable. Given her opinion, with no other evidence, she would have rejected the idea at once. She simply did not understand anything of a technical nature.

One day she bluntly asked him how he knew what he was doing.

James grinned. "I really *don't* know what I'm doing," he admitted. "I'm only following some very explicit directions. If I knew the pure theory of my father's machine I could not design the instrumentation that would make it work. But I can build a reproduction of my father's machine from the directions."

"How can that be?"

James stopped working and sat on a packing case. "If you bought a lawn-mower," he said, "it might come neatly packed in a little box with all the parts nested in cardboard formers and all the little nuts and bolts packed in a bag. There would be a set of assembly directions, written in such a way as to explain to anybody who can read that Part A is fastened to Bracket B using Bolt C, Lockwasher D, and Nut E. My father's one and only recognition of the dangers of the unforeseeable future was to drill deep in my brain these directions. For instance," and he pointed to a boxed device, "that thing is an infra-low frequency amplifier. Now, I haven't much more than a faint glimmer of what the thing is and how it differs from a standard amplifier, but I know that it must be built precisely thus-and-so, and finally it must be fitted into the machine per instructions. Look, Mrs. Bagley." James picked up a recently-received package, swept a place clear on the packing case and dumped it out. It disgorged several paper bags of parts, some large plates and a box. He handed her a booklet. "Try it yourself," he said. "That's a piece of test equipment made in kit form by a commercial outfit in Michigan. Follow those directions and build it for me."

"But I don't know anything about this sort of thing."

"You can read," said James with a complete lack of respect. He turned back to his own work, leaving Mrs. Bagley leafing her way through the assembly manual.

To the woman it was meaningless. But as she read, a secondary thought rose in her mind. James was building this devilish-looking nightmare, and he had every intention of using it on her daughter! She accepted without understanding the fact that James Holden's superior education had come of such a machine—but it had been a machine built by a competent mechanic. She stole a look at James. The anomaly puzzled her.

When the lad talked, his size and even the thin boyish voice were negated by the intelligence of his words, the size of his vocabulary, the clarity of his statements. Now that he was silent, he became no more than an eight-year-old lad who could not possibly be doing anything constructive with this mad array of equipment. The messiness of the place merely made the madness of the whole program seem worse.

But she turned back to her booklet. Maybe James was right. If she could assemble this doodad without knowing the first principle of its operation, without even knowing from the name what the thing did, then she might be willing to admit that—messy as it looked—the machine could be reconstructed.

Trapped by her own interest, Mrs. Bagley pitched in.

They took a week off to rearrange the place. They built wooden shelves to hold the parts in better order. These were by no means the work of a carpenter, for Mrs. Bagley's aim with a saw was haphazard, and her batting average with a hammer was about .470; but James lacked the strength, so the construction job was hers. Crude as it was, the place looked less like a junkshop when they were done. Work resumed on the assembly of the educator.

Of course the writing suffered.

The budget ran low. James was forced to abandon the project for his typewriter. He drove himself hard, fretting and worrying himself into a stew time after time. And then as August approached, Nature stepped in to add more disorder.

James entered a "period of growth." In three weeks he gained two inches.

His muscles, his bones and his nervous system ceased to coordinate. He became clumsy. His handwriting underwent a change, so severe that James had to practically forge his own signature of Charles Maxwell. To avoid trouble he stopped the practice of writing individual checks for the bills and transferred a block sum of money to an operating account in Mrs. Bagley's name.

His fine regimen went to pieces.

He embarked on a haphazard program of sleeping, eating and working at odd hours, and his appetite became positively voracious. He wanted what he wanted when he wanted it, even if it were the middle of the night. He pouted and groused when he didn't get it. In calmer moments he hated himself for these tantrums, but no amount of self-rationalization stopped them.

During this period, James was by no means an efficient youngster. His writing suffered the ills of both his period of growth and his upset state of mind. His fingers failed to coordinate on his typewriter and his manuscript copy turned out rough, with strikeovers, xxx-outs, and gross mistakes. The pile of discarded paper massed higher than his finished copy until Mrs. Bagley took over and began to retype his rough script for him.

His state of mind remained chaotic.

Mrs. Bagley began to treat him with special care.

She served him warm milk and insisted that he rest. Finally she asked him why he drove himself so hard.

"We are approaching the end of summer," he said, "and we are not prepared."

"Prepared for what?"

They were relaxing in the living room, James fretting and Mrs. Bagley seated, Martha Bagley asprawl on the floor turning the pages of a crayon-coloring book. "Look at us," he said. "I am a boy of eight, your daughter is a girl of seven. By careful dress and action I could pass for a child one year younger, but that would still make me seven. Last summer when I was seven, I passed for six."

"Yes, but—?"

"Mrs. Bagley, there are laws about compulsory education. Sooner or later someone is going to get very curious about us."

"What do you intend to do about it?"

"That's the problem," he said. "I don't really know. With a lot of concentrated effort I can probably enter school if I have to, and keep my education covered up. But Martha is another story."

"I don't see—?" Mrs. Bagley bit her lip.

"We can't permit her to attend school," said James.

"You shouldn't have advertised for a woman with a girl child!" said Mrs. Bagley.

"Perhaps not. But I wanted someone of my own age and size around so that we can grow together. I'm a bit of a misfit until I'm granted the right to use my education as I see fit."

"And you hope to make Martha another misfit?"

"If you care to put it that way," admitted James. "Someone has to start. Someday all kids will be educated with my machine and then there'll be no misfits."

"But until then—?"

"Mrs. Bagley, I am not worried about what is going to happen next year. I am worried about what is going to happen next month."

Mrs. Bagley sat and watched him for a moment. This boy was worried, she could see that. But assuming that any part of his story was true—and it was impossible to doubt it—he had ample cause.

The past years had given Mrs. Bagley a hard shell because it was useful for survival; to keep herself and her child alive she had had to be permanently alert for every threat. Clearly this was a threat. Martha was involved. Martha's future was, at the least, bound to be affected by what James did.

And the ties of blood and habit made Martha's future the first consideration in Janet Bagley's thoughts.

But not the only consideration; for there is an inborn trait in the human race which demands that any helpless child should be helped. James was hardly helpless; but he certainly was a child. It was easy to forget it, talking to him—until something came up that the child could not handle.

Mrs. Bagley sighed. In a different tone she asked, "What did you do last year?"

"Played with Rags on the lawn," James said promptly. "A boy and his dog is a perfectly normal sight—in the summer. Then, when school opened, I stayed in the house as much as I could. When I had to go out I tried to make myself look younger. Short pants, dirty face. I don't think I could get away with it this year."

"I think you're right," Mrs. Bagley admitted. "Well, suppose you could do what you wish this year? What would that be?"

James said: "I want to get my machine working. Then I want to use it on Martha."

"On Martha! But—"

James said patiently: "It won't hurt her, Mrs. Bagley. There isn't any other way. The first thing she needs is a good command of English."

"English?" Mrs. Bagley hesitated, and was lost. After all, what was wrong with the girl's learning proper speech?

"Martha is a child both physically and intellectually. She has been talked to about 'right' and 'wrong' and she knows that 'telling the truth' is right, but she doesn't recognize that talking about fairies is a misstatement of the truth. Question her carefully about how we live, and you'll get a fair approximation of the truth."

"So?"

"But suppose someone asks Martha about the Hermit of Martin's Hill?"

"What do you fear?"

"We might play upon her make-believe stronger than we have. She play-acts his existence very well. But suppose someone asks her what he eats, or where he gets his exercise, or some other personal question. She hasn't the command of logic to improvise a convincing background."

"But why should anybody ask such personal questions?" asked Mrs. Bagley.

James said patiently: "To ask personal questions of an adult is 'prying' and is therefore considered improper and antisocial. To ask the same questions of a child is proper and social. It indicates a polite interest in the world of the child. You and I, Mrs. Bagley, have a complete picture of the Hermit all prepared, and with our education we can improvise plausible answers. I've hoped to finish my machine early enough to provide Martha with the ability to do the same."

"So what can we do?"

"About the only thing we can do is to hide," said James. "Luckily, most of the business is conducted out of this place by mail. Write letters to some boarding school situated a good many miles from here. Ask the usual routine questions about entering a seven-year-old girl and an eight-year-old boy for one semester. Robert Holmes, our postmaster-taxicab driver-station-master, reads everything that isn't sealed. He will read the addresses, and he will see replies and read their return address."

"And then we'll pretend to send you and Martha to boarding school?"

James nodded. "Confinement is going to be difficult, but in this climate the weather gets nasty early and that keeps people out of one another's hair."

"But this station-master business—?"

"We've got to pull some wool over Robert's eyes," said James. "Somehow, we've got to make it entirely plausible. You've got to take Martha and me away and come back alone just as if we were in school."

"We should have a car," said Mrs. Bagley.

"A car is one piece of hardware that I could never justify," said James. "Nor," he chuckled, "buy from a mail-order house because I couldn't accept delivery. I bought furniture from Sears and had it delivered according to mailed instructions. But I figured it better to have the folks in Shipmont wondering why Charles Maxwell didn't own a car than to have them puzzling why he owned one that never was used, nor even moved. Besides, a car—costs—"

Mrs. Bagley smiled with real satisfaction. "There," she said, "I think I can help. I can buy the car."

James was startled. "But can you afford it?"

Mrs. Bagley nodded seriously. "James," she said, "I've been scratching out an existence on hard terms and I've had to make sure of tomorrow. Even when things were worst, I tried to put something away— some weeks it was only a few pennies, sometimes nothing at all. But—well, I'm not afraid of tomorrow any more."

James was oddly pleased. While he was trying to find a way to say it, Mrs. Bagley relieved him of the necessity. "It won't be a brand-new convertible," she warned. "But they tell me you can get something that runs for two or three hundred dollars. Tim Fisher has some that look about right in his garage—and besides," she said, clinching it, "it gives me a chance to give out a little more Maxwell and boarding-school propaganda."

CHAPTER NINE

The letter was a masterpiece of dissembling. It suggested, without promising, that Charles Maxwell intended to send his young charge to boarding school along with his housekeeper's daughter. It asked the school's advice and explained the deformity that made Charles Maxwell a recluse. The reply could hardly have been better if they'd penned it themselves for the signature of the faculty advisor. It discussed the pros and cons of away-from-home schooling and went on at great length to discuss the attitude of children and their upbringing amid strange surroundings. It invited a long and inconclusive correspondence—just what James wanted.

The supposed departure for school went off neatly, no one in the town of Shipmont was surprised when Mrs. Bagley turned up buying an automobile of several years' vintage because this was a community where everybody had one.

The letters continued at the rate of one every two or three weeks. They were picked up by Mrs. Bagley who let it be known that these were progress reports. In reality, they were little tracts on the theory of child education. They kept up the correspondence for the information it contained, and also because Mrs. Bagley enjoyed this contact with an outer world that contained adults.

Meanwhile, James ended his spurt of growth and settled down. Work on his machine continued when he could afford to buy the parts, and his writing settled down into a comfortable channel once more. In his spare time James began to work on Martha's diction.

Martha could not have been called a retarded child. Her trouble was lack of constant parental attention during her early years. With father gone and mother struggling to live, Martha had never overcome some of the babytalk-diction faults. There was still a trace of the omitted 'B' here and there. 'Y' was a difficult sound; the color of a lemon was "Lellow." Martha's English construction still bore marks of the baby. "Do you have to—" came out as "Does you has to—?"

James Holden's father had struggled in just this way through his early experimental days, when he despaired of ever getting the infant James out of the baby-prattle stage. He could not force, he could not even coerce. All that his father could do was to watch quietly as baby James acquired the awareness of things. Then he could step in and supply the correct word-sound to name the object. In those early days the progress of James Holden was no greater than the progress of any other infant. Holden Senior followed the theory of ciphers; no cryptologist can start unravelling a secret message until he is aware of the fact that some hidden message exists. No infant can be taught a language until some awareness tells the tiny brain that there is some definite connection between sound and sight.

For the next few weeks James worked with Martha on her speech, and hated it. So slow, so dreary! But it was necessary, he thought, to keep her from establishing any more permanent errors, so that when the machine was ready there would be at least a blank slate to write on, not one all scribbled over with mistakes.

Time passed; the weather grew colder; the machine spread its scattered parts over his workroom.

Janet Bagley knew that the machine was growing, but it had not occurred to her that it would be finished. She had grown accustomed to her life on Martin's Hill. By her standards, it was easy. She made three meals each day, cleaned the rooms, hung curtains, sewed clothing for Martha and herself, did the shopping and had time enough left over to take excursions in her little car and keep her daughter out of mischief. It was pleasant. It was more than pleasant, it was safe.

And then the machine was finished.

Mrs. Bagley took a sandwich and a glass of milk to James and found him sitting on a chair, a heavy headset covering most of his skull, reading aloud from a textbook on electronic theory.

Mrs. Bagley stopped at the door, unaccountably startled.

James looked up and shut off his work. "It's finished," he said with grave pride.

"All of it?"

"Well," he said, pondering, "the basic part. It works."

Mrs. Bagley looked at the scramble of equipment in the room as though it were an enemy. It didn't *look* finished. It didn't even look safe. But she trusted James, although she felt at that moment that she would grow old and die before she understood why and how any collection of apparatus could be functional and still be so untidy. "It—could teach me?"

"If you had something you want to memorize."

"I'd like to memorize some of the pet recipes from my cookbook."

"Get it," directed James.

She hesitated. "How does it work?" she wanted to know first.

He countered with another question. "How do we memorize anything?"

She thought. "Why, by repeating and repeating and rehearsing and rehearsing."

"Yes," said James. "So this device does the repetition for you. Electromechanically."

"But how?"

James smiled wistfully. "I can give you only a thumbnail sketch," he said, "until I have had time to study the subjects that lead up to the final theory."

"Goodness," exclaimed Mrs. Bagley, "all I want is a brief idea. I wouldn't understand the principles at all."

"Well, then, my mother, as a cerebral surgeon, knew the anatomy of the human brain. My father, as an instrument-maker, designed and built encephalographs. Together, they discovered that if the great waves of the brain were filtered down and the extremely minute waves that ride on top of them were amplified, the pattern of these superfine waves went through convolutions peculiar to certain thoughts. Continued research refined their discovery.

"Now, the general theory is that the cells of the brain act sort of like a binary digital computer, with certain banks of cells operating to store sufficient bits of information to furnish a complete memory. In the process of memorization, individual cells become activated and linked by the constant repetition.

"Second, the brain within the skull is a prisoner, connected to the 'outside' by the five standard sensory channels of sight, sound, touch, taste, and smell. Stimulate a channel, and the result is a certain waveshape of electrical impulse that enters the brain and—sort of like the key to a Yale lock—fits only one combination of cells. Or if no previous memory is there, it starts its own new collection of cells to linking and combining. When we repeat and repeat, we are deepening the groove, so to speak.

"Finally comes the Holden Machine. The helmet makes contact with the skull in those spots where the probes of the encephalograph are placed. When the brain is stimulated into thought, the brain waves are monitored and recorded, amplified, and then fed back to the same brain-spots. Not once, but multifold, like the vibration of a reed or violin string. The circuit that accepts signals, amplifies them, returns them to the same set of terminals, and causes them to be repeated several hundred times per millisecond without actually ringing or oscillating is the real research secret of the machine. My father's secret and now mine."

"And how do we use it?"

"You want to memorize a list of ingredients," said James. "So you will put this helmet on your head with the cookbook in your hands. You will turn on the machine when you have read the part you want to memorize just to be sure of your material. Then, with the machine running, you carefully read aloud the passage from your book. The vibrating amplifier in the machine monitors and records each electrical impulse, then furnishes it back to your brain as a successive series of repetitious vibrations, each identical in shape and magnitude, just as if you had actually read and re-read that list of stuff time and again."

"And then I'll know it cold?"

James shook his head. "Then you'll be about as confused as you've ever been. For several hours, none of it will make sense. You'll be thinking things like a 'cup of salt and a pinch of water,' or maybe, 'sugar three of mustard and two spoonthree teas.' And then in a few hours all of this mishmash will settle itself down into the proper serial arrangement; it will fit the rest of your brain-memory-pattern comfortably."

"Why?"

"I don't know. It has something to do with the same effect one gets out of studying. On Tuesday one can read a page of textbook and not grasp a word of it. Successive readings help only a little. Then in about a week it all becomes quite clear, just as if the brain had sorted it and filed it logically among the other bits of information. Well, what about that cookbook?"

"Yes," said Mrs. Bagley, with the air of someone agreeing to have a tooth pulled when it hasn't really started to hurt, "I'll get it."

James Holden allowed himself a few pleasant daydreams. The most satisfactory of all was one of himself pleading his own case before the black-robed Justices of the Supreme Court, demolishing his detractors with a flow of his brilliance and convincing them beyond any doubt that he did indeed have the right to walk alone. That there be no question of his intellect, James proposed to use his machine to educate himself to completion. He would be the supreme student of the arts and the sciences, of law, language, and literature. He would know history and the humanities, and the dreams and aims of the great philosophers and statesmen, and he would even be able to quote in their own terms the drives of the great dictators and some of the evil men so that he could draw and compare to show that he knew the difference between good and bad.

But James Holden had no intention of sharing this limelight.

His superb brilliance was to be compared to the average man's, not to another one like him. He had the head start. He intended to keep it until he had succeeded in compelling the whole world to accept him with the full status of a free adult.

Then, under his guidance, he would permit the worldwide use of his machine.

His loneliness had forced him to revise that dream by the addition of Martha Bagley; he needed a companion, contemporary, and foil. His mental playlet no longer closed with James Holden standing alone before the Bench. Now it ended with Martha saying proudly, "James, I knew you could do it."

Martha Bagley's brilliance would not conflict with his. He could stay ahead of her forever. But he had no intention of allowing some experienced adult to partake of this program of enforced education. He was, therefore, going to find himself some manner or means of preventing Mrs. Bagley from running the gamut of all available information.

James Holden evaluated all people in his own terms, he believed that everybody was just as eager for knowledge as he was.

So he was surprised to find that Mrs. Bagley's desire for extended education only included such information as would make her own immediate personal problems easier. Mrs. Bagley was the first one of the mass of people James was destined to meet who not only did not know how or why things worked, but further had no intention whatsoever of finding out.

Instead of trying to monopolize James Holden's machine, Mrs. Bagley was satisfied to learn a number of her pet recipes. After a day of thought she added her social security number, blood type, some birthdays, dates, a few telephone numbers and her multiplication tables. She announced that she was satisfied. It solved James Holden's problem—and stunned him completely.

But James had very little time to worry about Mrs. Bagley's attitude. He found his hands full with Martha.

Martha played fey. Her actions and attitude baffled James, and even confused her mother. There was no way of really determining whether the girl was scared to death of the machine itself, or whether she simply decided to be difficult. And she uttered the proper replies with all of the promptness—and intelligence—of a ventriloquist's dummy:

"You don't want to be ignorant, do you?"

"No."

"You want to be smart, like James, don't you?"

"Yes."

"You know the machine won't hurt, don't you?"

"Yes."

"Then let's try it just once, please?"

"No."

Back to the beginning again. Martha would agree to absolutely anything except the educator.

Leaving the argument to Mrs. Bagley, James sat down angrily with a book. He was so completely frustrated that he couldn't read, but he sat there leafing the pages slowing and making a determined show of not lifting his head.

Mrs. Bagley went on for another hour before she reached the end of her own patience. She stood up almost rigid with anger. James never knew how close Mrs. Bagley was to making use of a hairbrush on her daughter's bottom. But Mrs. Bagley also realized that Martha had to go into this process willing to cooperate. So, instead of physical punishment, she issued a dictum:

"You'll go to your room and stay there until you're willing!"

And at that point Martha ceased being stubborn and began playing games.

She permitted herself to be led to the chair, and then went through a routine of skittishness, turning her head and squirming incessantly, which made it impossible for James to place the headset properly. This went on until he stalked away and sat down again. Immediately Martha sat like a statue. But as soon as James reached for the little screws that adjusted the electrodes, Martha started to giggle and squirm. He stalked away and sat through another session between Martha and her mother.

Late in the afternoon James succeeded in getting her to the machine; Martha uttered a sentence without punctuating it with little giggles, but it came as elided babytalk.

"Again," he commanded.

"I don't wan' to."

"Again!" he snapped.

Martha began to cry.

That, to James, was the end. But Mrs. Bagley

stepped forward with a commanding wave for James to vacate the premises and took over. James could not analyze her expression, but it did look as if it held relief. He left the room to them; a half hour later Mrs. Bagley called him back.

"She's had it," said Mrs. Bagley. "Now you can start, I think."

James looked dubious; but said, "Read this."

"Martha?"

Martha took a deep breath and said, nicely, " 'A' is the first letter of the English Alphabet."

"Good." He pressed the button. "Again? Please?"

Martha recited it nicely.

"Fine," he said. "Now we'll look up 'Is' and go on from there."

"My goodness," said Mrs. Bagley, "this is going to take months."

"Not at all," said James. "It just goes slowly at the start. Most of the definitions use the same words over and over again. Martha really knows most of these simple words, we've just got to be dead certain that her own definition of them agrees wholly and completely with ours. After a couple of hours of this minute detail, we'll be skipping over everything but new words. After all, she only has to work them over once, and as we find them, we'll mark them out of the book. Ready, Martha?"

"Can't read it."

James took the little dictionary. "Um," he said. "Hadn't occurred to me."

"What?" asked Mrs. Bagley.

"This thing says, Three-rd pers period sing periodic indic period of Be,' the last in heavy bold type. Can't have Martha talking in abbreviations," he chuckled. He went to the typewriter and wrote it out fully. "Now read that," he directed.

She did and again the process went through without a hitch. Slowly, but surely, they progressed for almost two hours before Martha rebelled. James stopped, satisfied with the beginning.

But as time wore on into the late autumn, Martha slowly—oh, so slowly!—began to realize that there was importance to getting things right. She continued to tease. But she did her teasing before James closed the "Run" button.

CHAPTER TEN

Once James progressed Martha through the little dictionary, he began with a book of grammar. Again it started slowly; he had to spend quite a bit of time explaining to Martha that she did indeed know all of the terms used in the book of grammar because they'd all been defined by the dictionary, now she was going to learn how the terms and their definitions were used.

James was on more familiar ground now. James, like Martha, had learned his first halting sentence structure by mimicking his parents, but he remembered the process of learning why and how sentences are constructed according to the rules, and how the rules are used rather than intuition in forming sentences.

Grammar was a topic that could not be taken in snippets and bits. Whole paragraphs had to be read until Martha could read them without a halt or a mispronunciation, and then committed to memory with the "Run" button held down. At the best it was a boring process, even though it took only minutes instead of days. It was not conflicting, but it was confusing. It installed permanently certain solid blocks of information that were isolated; they stood alone until later blocks came in to connect them into a whole area.

Each session was numbing. Martha could take no more than a couple of hours, after which her reading became foggy. She wanted a nap after each session and even after the nap she went around in a bemused state of mental dizziness.

Life settled down once more in the House on Martin's Hill. James worked with the machine himself and laid out lessons to guide Martha. Then, finished for the day with education, James took to his typewriter while Martha had her nap. It filled the days of the boy and girl completely.

This made an unexpected and pleasant change in Mrs. Bagley's routine. It had been a job to keep Martha occupied. Now that Martha was busy, Mrs. Bagley found time on her own hands; without interruption, her housework routine was completed quite early in the afternoon.

Mrs. Bagley had never made any great point of getting dressed for dinner. She accumulated a collection of house-frocks; printed cotton washables differing somewhat in color and cut but functionally identical. She wore them serially as they came from the row of hangers in her closet.

Now she began to acquire some dressier things, wearing them even during her shopping trips.

James paid little attention to this change in his housekeeper's routine, but he approved. Mrs. Bagley was also taking more pains with the 'do' of her hair, but the boy's notice was not detailed enough to take a part-by-section inventory of the whole. In fact, James gave the whole matter very little thought until Mrs. Bagley made a second change after her return from town, appearing for dinner in what James could only classify as a party dress.

She asked, "James, do you mind if I go out this evening?"

James, startled, shrugged and said. "No, I guess not."

"You'll keep an ear out for Martha?"

The need for watching a sleeping girl of seven and a half did not penetrate. "What's up?" he asked.

"It's been months since I saw a movie."

James shrugged again, puzzled. "You saw the 'Bride of Frankenstein' last night on TV," he pointed out.

"I first saw that old horror when I was about your age," she told him with a trace of disdain.

"I liked it."

"So did I at eight and a half. But tonight I'm going to see a *new* picture."

"Okay," said James, wondering why anybody in their right mind would go out on a chilly night late in November just to see a moving picture when they could stay at home and watch one in comfort. "Have a good time."

He expected Mrs. Bagley to take off in her car, but she did not. She waited until a brief *toot!* came from the road. Then, with a swirl of motion, she left.

It took James Holden's limited experience some little time to identify the event with some similar scenes from books he'd read; even with him, reading about it was one world and seeing it happen was another thing entirely.

For James Holden it opened a new area for contemplation. He would have to know something about this matter if he hoped to achieve his dreamed-of status as an adult.

Information about the relation between man and woman had not been included in the course of education devised by his father and mother. Therefore his physical age and his information on the delicate subject were approximately parallel.

His personal evaluation of the subject was uncomplicated. At some age not much greater than his own, boys and girls conglomerated in a mass that milled around in a constant state of flux and motion, like individual atoms of gas compressed in a container. Meetings and encounters took place both singly and in groups until nearly everybody had been in touch with almost everybody else. Slowly the amorphous mass changed. Groups became attracted by mutual interests. Changes and exchanges took place, and then a pair-formation began to take place. The pair-formation went through its interchanges both with and without friction as the settling-down process proceeded. At times predictable by comparing it to the statistics of radioactivity, the pair-production resulted in permanent combination, which effectively removed this couple from free circulation.

James Holden had no grasp or feeling for the great catalyst that causes this pair-production; he saw it only for its sheer mechanics. To him, the sensible way to go about this matter was to get there early and move fast, because one stands to make a better choice when there is a greater number of unattached specimens from which to choose. Those left over are likely to have flaws.

And so he pondered, long after Martha had gone to bed.

He was still up and waiting when he heard the car stop at the gate. He watched them come up the walk arm in arm, their stride slow and lingering. They paused for several moments on the doorstep, once there was a short, muted laugh. The snick of the key came next and they came into the hallway.

"No, please don't come in," said Mrs. Bagley.

"But—" replied the man.

"But me no buts. It's late, Tim."

Tim? Tim? That would probably be Timothy Fisher. He ran the local garage where Mrs. Bagley bought her car. James went on listening shamelessly.

"Late? Phooey. When is eleven-thirty late?"

"When it's right now," she replied with a light laugh. "Now, Tim. It's been very —"

There came a long silence.

Her voice was throaty when the silence broke. "Now, will you go?"

"Of course," he said.

"Not that way, silly," she said. "The door's behind you."

"Isn't the door I want," he chuckled.

"We're making enough noise to wake the dead," she complained.

"Then let's stop talking," he told her.

There was another long silence.

"Now please go."

"Can I come back tomorrow night?"

"Not tomorrow."

"Friday?"

"Saturday."

"It's a date, then."

"All right. Now get along with you."

"You're cruel and heartless, Janet," he complained. "Sending a man out in that cold and storm."

"It isn't storming, and you've a fine heater in that car of yours."

"I'd rather have you."

"Do you tell that to all the girls?"

"Sure. Even Maggie the Washerwoman is better than an old car heater."

Mrs. Bagley chuckled throatily. "How is Maggie?"

"She's fine."

"I mean as a date."

"Better than the car heater."

"Tim, you're a fool."

"When I was a kid," said Tim reflectively, "there used to be a female siren in the movies. Her pet line used to be 'Kiss me, my fool!' Theda Bara, I think. Before talkies. Now—"

"No, Tim—"

Another long silence.

"Now, Tim, you've simply *got* to go!"

"Yeah, I know. You've convinced me."

"Then why aren't you going?"

He chuckled. "Look, you've convinced me. I can't stay so I'll go, obviously. But now that we've covered this problem, let's drop the subject for a while, huh?"

"Don't spoil a fine evening, Tim."

"Janet, what's with you, anyway?"

"What do you mean, 'what's with me?' "

"Just this. Somewhere up in the house is this oddball Maxwell who hides out all the time. He's either asleep or busy. Anyway, he isn't here. Do you have to report in, punch a time clock, tuck him in—or do you turn into a pumpkin at the stroke of twelve?"

"Mr. Maxwell is paying me wages to keep house for him. That's all. Part of my wages is my keep. But it doesn't entitle me to have full run of the house or to bring guests in at midnight for a two-hour good-night session."

"I'd like to tell this bird a thing or two," said Tim Fisher sharply. "He can't keep you cooped up like—like—"

"Nobody is keeping me cooped up," she said. "Like what?"

"What?"

"You said 'like—' "

"Skip it. What I meant is that you can't moulder, Janet. You've got to get out and meet people."

"I've been out and I've met people. I've met you."

"All to the good."

"Fine. So you invited me out, and I went. It was fun. I liked it. You've asked me, and I've said that I'd like to do it again on Saturday. I've enjoyed being kissed, and I'll probably enjoy it again on Saturday. So—"

"I'd think you'd enjoy a lot of it."

"Because my husband has been gone for five years?"

"Oh, now Janet—"

"That's what you meant, isn't it?"

"No. You've got me wrong."

"Tim, stop it. You're spoiling a fine evening. You should have gone before it started to spoil. Now please put your smile on again and leave cheerfully. There's always Saturday—if you still want it."

"I'll call you," he said.

The door opened once more and then closed. James took a deep breath, and then stole away quietly to his own room.

By some instinct he knew that this was no time to intercept Mrs. Bagley with a lot of fool questions.

To the surprise and puzzlement of young James Quincy Holden, Mr. Timothy Fisher telephoned early upon the following evening. He was greeted quite cordially by Mrs. Bagley. Their conversation was rambling and inane, especially when heard from one end only, and it took them almost ten minutes to confirm their Saturday night date. That came as another shock.

Well, not quite. The explanation bothered him even more than the fact itself. As a further extension of his little mechanical mating process, James had to find a place for the like of Jake Caslow and the women Jake knew. None of them were classed in the desirable group, all of them were among the leftovers. But of course, since none of them were good enough for the 'good' people, they were good enough for one another, and that made it all right—for them.

But Mrs. Bagley was not of their ilk. It was not right that she should be forced to take a leftover.

And then it occurred to him that perhaps Mrs. Bagley was not really taking the leftover, Tim Fisher, but instead was using Tim Fisher's company as a means toward meeting a larger group, from which there might be a better specimen. So he bided his time, thinking deeply around the subject, about which he knew nothing whatsoever.

Saturday night was a repeat of Wednesday. They stayed out later, and upon their return they took possession of the living room for at least an hour before they started their routine about the going-home process. With minor variations in the dialog, and with longer and more frequent silences, it almost followed the Wednesday night script. The variation puzzled James even more. This session went according to program for a while until Tim Fisher admitted with regret that it was, indeed, time for him to depart. At which juncture Mrs. Bagley did not leap to her feet to accept his offer to do that which she had been asking him to do for a half hour. Mrs. Bagley compounded the affair by sighing deeply and agreeing with him that it was a shame that it was so late and that she, too, wished that he could stay a little longer. This, of course, put them precisely where they were a half hour earlier and they had to start the silly business all over again.

They parted after a final fifteen-minute discussion at the front door. This discussion covered Sunday, Monday, Tuesday, and finally came to agreement on Wednesday.

And so James Holden went to bed that night fully convinced that in a town of approximately two thousand people—he did not count the two or three hundred A.E.C.-College group as part of the problem—there were entirely too few attractive leftovers from which Mrs. Bagley could choose.

But as this association grew, it puzzled him even more. For in his understanding, any person forced to accept a second-rate choice does so with an air of resignation, but not with a cheerful smile, a sparkle in the eyes, and two hours of primping.

James sought the answer in his books but they were the wrong volumes for reference of this subject. He considered the local Public Library only long enough to remember that it carried a few hundred books suitable for the A.E.C.-College crew and a thousand or so of second-hand culls donated by local citizens during clean-up campaigns. He resorted to buying books by mail through advertisements in newspapers and magazines and received a number of volumes of medical treatises, psychological texts, and a book on obstetrics that convinced him that baby-having was both rare and hazardous. He read *By Love Possessed* but he did not recognize the many forms of love portrayed by the author because the volume was not annotated with signs or provided with a road map, and he did not know it when he read about it.

He went through the Kinsey books and absorbed a lot of data and graphs and figures on human behavior that meant nothing to him. James was not even interested in the incidence of homosexuality among college students as compared to religious groups, or in the comparison between premarital experience and level of education. He knew the words and what the words meant as defined in other words. But they were only words and did not touch him where he lived.

So, because none of the texts bothered to explain why a woman says Yes, when she means No, nor why a woman will cling to a man's lapels and press herself against him and at the same time tell him he has to go home, James remained ignorant. He could have learned more from Lord Byron, Shelley, Keats, or Browning than from Kinsey, deLee, or the "Instructive book on Sex, forwarded under plain wrapper for $2.69 postpaid."

Luckily for James, he did not study any of his material via the medium of his father's machine or it would have made him sick. For he was not yet capable of understanding the single subject upon which more words have been expended in saying less than any other subject since the dawn of history.

His approach was academic, he could have been reading the definitive material on the life-cycle of the beetle insofar as any stir of his own blood was concerned.

From his study he did identify a couple of items. Tim Fisher obviously desired extramarital relations with Mrs. Bagley—or was it premarital relations? Probably both. Logic said that Mrs. Bagley, having already been married to Martha's father, could hardly enter into *pre*marital relations, although Tim could, since he was a bachelor. But they wouldn't be *pre*-

marital with Tim unless he followed through and married Mrs. Bagley. And so they must be *extra*marital. But whatever they were called, the Book said that there was about as much on one side as on the other.

With a mind mildly aware of the facts of life, distorted through the eyes of near-nine James Holden, he watched them and listened in.

As for Mrs. Bagley, she did not know that she was providing part of James Holden's extraliterary education. She enjoyed the company of Tim Fisher. Hesitantly, she asked James if she could have Tim for dinner one evening, and was a bit surprised at his immediate assent. They planned the evening, cleaned the lower part of the house of every trace of its current occupancy, and James and Martha hied themselves upstairs. Dinner went with candlelight and charcoal-broiled steak—and a tray taken aloft for "Mr. Maxwell" was consumed by James and Martha. The evening went smoothly. They listened to music and danced, they sat and talked. And James listened.

Tim was not the same man. He sat calm and comfortably on the low sofa with Mrs. Bagley's head on his shoulder, both of them pleasantly bemused by the dancing fireplace and with each other's company. He said, "Well, I'm glad this finally happened."

"What happened?" she replied in a murmur.

"Getting the invite for dinner."

"Might have been sooner, I suppose. Sorry."

"What took you so long?"

"Just being cautious, I guess."

He chuckled. "Cautious?"

"Uh-huh."

Tim laughed.

"What's so darned funny?"

"Women."

"Are we such a bunch of clowns?"

"Not clowns, Janet. Just funny."

"All right, genius. Explain that."

"A woman is a lovely creature who sends a man

away so that he can't do what she wants him to do most of all."

"Uh-huh."

"She feeds him full of rare steak until he wants to crawl off in a corner like the family mutt and go to sleep. Once she gets him in a somnolent state, she drapes herself tastefully on his shoulder and gets soft and warm and willing."

Mrs. Bagley laughed throatily. "Just start getting active," she warned, "and you'll see how fast I can beat a hasty retreat."

"Janet, what *is* with you?"

"What do you mean?"

"What are you hiding?"

"Hiding?"

"Yes, confound it, hiding!" he said, his voice turning hard. "Just who is this Charles Maxwell character, anyway?"

"Tim, please—"

His voice lowered again. "Janet," he said softly, "you're asking me to trust you, and at the same time you're not trusting me."

"But I've nothing to hide."

"Oh, stop it. I'm no schoolboy, Janet. If you have nothing to hide, why are you acting as if you were sitting on the lid?"

"I still don't know what you're talking about."

"Your words say so, but your tone is the icy haughtiness that dares me, mere male that I am, to call your lie. I've a half-notion to stomp upstairs and confront your mysterious Maxwell—if he indeed exists."

"You mustn't. He'd—"

"He'd what? I've been in this house for hours day and night and now all evening. I've never heard a sound, not the creak of a floorboard, the slam of a door, the opening of a window, nor the distant gurgle of cool, clear water, gushing into plumbing. So you've been married. This I know. You have a daughter. This I accept. Your husband is dead. This happens to people every day; nice people, bad people, bright people, dull people. There was a young boy here last summer. Him I do not know, but you and your daughter I do know about. I've checked—"

"How dare you check—?"

"I damn well dare check anything and anybody I happen to be personally interested in," he stormed. "As a potential bed partner I wouldn't give a hoot who you were or what you were. But before I go to the point of dividing the rest of my life on an exclusive contract, I have the right to know what I'm splitting it with."

"You have no right—"

"Balderdash! I have as much right as anybody to look at the record. I grant you the same right to look up my family and my friends and the status of my bank account and my credit rating and my service record. Grant it? Hell, I couldn't stop you. Now, what's going on? Where is your daughter and where is that little boy? And where—if he exists—is this Charles Maxwell?"

James had heard enough. No matter which way this was going, it would end up wrong. He was proud of Mrs. Bagley's loyalty, but he knew that it was an increasing strain and could very well lead to complications that could not be explained away without the whole truth. He decided that the only thing to do was to put in his own oar and relieve Mrs. Bagley.

He walked in, yawning. He stood between them, facing Tim Fisher. Behind him, Mrs. Bagley cried, "Now see—you've awakened him!"

In a dry-throated voice, Tim said, "I thought he was away at school. Now, what's the story?"

"It isn't her story to tell," said James. "It's mine."

"Now see here—"

"Mr. Fisher, you can't learn anything by talking incessantly."

Tim Fisher took a step forward, his face dark, his

intention to shake the truth out of somebody. James held up a hand. "Sit down a moment and listen," he ordered.

The sight of James and the words that this child was uttering stopped Tim Fisher. Puzzled, he nodded dumbly, found a chair, and sat on the front edge of it, poised.

"The whereabouts of Mr. Maxwell is his own business and none of yours. Your criticism is unfounded and your suspicions unworthy. But since you take the attitude that this is some of your business, we don't mind telling you that Mr. Maxwell is in New York on business."

Tim Fisher eyed the youngster. "I thought you were away at school," he repeated.

"I heard you the first time," said James. "Obviously, I am not. Why I am not is Mr. Maxwell's business, not yours. And by insisting that something is wrong here and demanding the truth, you have placed Mrs. Bagley in the awkward position of having to make a decision that divides her loyalties. She has had the complete trust of Mr. Maxwell for almost a year and a half. Now, tell me, Mr. Fisher, to whom shall she remain loyal?"

"That isn't the point—"

"Yes, it is the point, Mr. Fisher. It is exactly the point. You're asking Mrs. Bagley to tell you the details of her employer's business, which is unethical."

"How much have you heard?" demanded Fisher crossly.

"Enough, at least to know what you've been hammering at."

"Then you know that I've as much as said that there was some suspicion attached."

"Suspicion of what?"

"Well, why aren't you in school?"

"That's Mr. Maxwell's business."

"Let me tell you, youngster, it is more than your

Mr. Maxwell's business. There are laws about education and he's breaking them."

James said patiently: "The law states that every child shall receive an adequate education. The precise wording I do not know, but it does provide for schooling outside of the state school system if the parent or guardian so prefers, and providing that such extraschool education is deemed adequate by the state. Can you say that I am not properly educated, Mr. Fisher?"

"Well, you'd hardly expect me to be an expert on the subject."

"Then I'd hardly expect you to pass judgment, either," said James pointedly.

"You're pretty—" Tim Fisher caught his tongue at the right moment. He felt his neck getting hot. It is hard enough to be told that you are off-base and that your behavior has been bad when an adult says the damning words. To hear the same words from a ten-year-old is unbearable. Right or wrong, the adult's position is to turn aside or shut the child up either by pulling rank or cuffing the young offender with an open hand. To have this upstart defend Mrs. Bagley, in whose presence he could hardly lash back, put Mr. Fisher in a very unhappy state of mind. He swallowed and then asked, lamely, "Why does he have to be so furtive?"

"What is your definition of 'furtive'?" asked James calmly. "Do you employ the same term to describe the operations of that combination College-A.E.C. installation on the other side of town?"

"That's secret—"

"Implying that atomic energy is secretly aboveboard, legal, and honorable, whereas Mr. Maxwell's—"

"But we know about atomic energy."

"Sure we do," jeered James, and the sound of his immature near-treble voice made the jeer very close to an insult. "We know *all* about atomic energy. Was the Manhattan Project called 'furtive' until Hiroshima gave the story away?"

"You're trying to put words in my mouth," objected Tim.

"No, I'm not. I'm merely trying to make you understand something important to everybody. You come in here and claim by the right of personal interest that we should be most willing to tell you our business. Then in the next breath you defend the installation over on the other side of town for their attitude in giving the bum's rush to people who try to ask questions about their business. Go read your Constitution, Mr. Fisher. It says there that I have as much right to defend my home against intruders as the A.E.C. has to defend their home against spies."

"But I'm not intruding."

James nodded his head gently. "Not," he said, "until you make the grave error of equating personal privacy with culpable guilt."

"I didn't mean that."

"You should learn to say what you mean," said James, "instead of trying to pry information out of someone who happens to be fond of you."

"Now see here," said Tim Fisher, "I happen to be fond of her too, you know. Doesn't that give me some rights?"

"Would you expect to know all of her business if she were your wife?"

"Of course."

"Suppose she were working in the A.E.C.-College?"

"Well, that—er—"

"Would be different?"

"Well, now—"

"I talked this right around in its circle for a purpose," said James. "Stop and think for a moment. Let's discuss me. Mr. Fisher, where would you place me in school?"

"Er—how old are you?"

"Nine," said James. "In April."

"Well, I'm not sure—"

"Exactly. Do you suppose that I could sit in a classroom among my nine-year-old contemporaries very long without being found out?"

"Er—no—I suppose not."

"Mr. Fisher, how long do you think I could remain a secret if I attended high school, sitting at a specially installed desk in a class among teenagers twice my size?"

"Not very long."

"Then remember that some secrets are so big that you have to have armed guards to keep them secret, and others are so easy to conceal that all you need is a rambling old house and a plausible façade."

"Why have you told me all this?"

"Because you have penetrated this far by your own effort, justified by your own personal emotions, and driven by an urge that is all-powerful if I am to believe the books I've read on the subject. You are told this much of the truth so that you won't go off half-cocked with a fine collection of rather dangerous untruths. Understand?"

"I'm beginning to."

"Well, whether Mrs. Bagley accepts your offer of marriage or not, remember one thing: If she were working for the A.E.C. you'd be proud of her, and you'd also be quite careful not to ask questions that would cause her embarrassment."

Tim Fisher looked at Mrs. Bagley. "Well?" he asked.

Mrs. Bagley looked bleak. "Please don't ask me until I've had a chance to discuss all of the angles with Mr. Maxwell, Tim."

"Maxwell, again."

"Tim," she said in a quiet voice, "remember—he's an employer, not an emotional involvement."

James Holden looked at Tim Fisher. "And if you'll promise to keep this thing as close a secret as you would some information about atomic energy, I'll go to bed and let you settle your personal problems in private. Good night!"

He left, reasonably satisfied that Tim Fisher would probably keep their secret for a time, at least. The hinted suggestion that this was as important a government project as the Atomic Energy Commission's works would prevent casual talk. There was also the slim likelihood that Tim Fisher might enjoy the position of being on the inside of a big secret, although this sort of inner superiority lacks true satisfaction. There was a more solid chance that Tim Fisher, being the ambitious man that he was, would keep their secret in the hope of acquiring for himself some of the superior knowledge and the advanced ability that went with it.

But James was certain that the program that had worked so well with Mrs. Bagley would fail with Tim Fisher. James had nothing material to offer Tim. Tim was the kind of man who would insist upon his wife being a full-time wife, physically, emotionally, and intellectually.

And James suddenly realized that Tim Fisher's own ambition and character would insist that Mrs. Bagley, with Martha, leave James Holden to take up residence in a home furnished by Tim Fisher upon the date and at time she became Mrs. Timothy Fisher.

He was still thinking about the complications this would cause when he heard Tim leave. His clock said three-thirty.

James Holden's mechanical educator was a wonderful machine, but there were some aspects of knowledge that it was not equipped to impart. The glandular comprehension of love was one such; there were others. In all of his hours under the machine James had not learned how personalities change and grow.

And yet there was a textbook case right before his eyes.

In a few months, Janet Bagley had changed from a frightened and belligerent mother-animal to a cheerful young prospective wife. The importance of the change lay in the fact that it was not polar, nothing reversed; it was only that the emphasis passed gradually from the protection of the young to the development of Janet Bagley herself.

James could not very well understand, though he tried, but he couldn't miss seeing it happen. It was worrisome. It threatened complications.

There was quite a change that came with Tim Fisher's elevation in status from steady date to affianced husband, heightened by Tim Fisher's partial understanding of the situation at Martin's Hill.

Then, having assumed the right to drop in as he pleased, he went on to assume more "rights" as Mrs. Bagley's fiancé. He brought in his friends from time to time. Not without warning, of course, for he understood the need for secrecy. When he brought friends it was after warning, and very frequently after he had helped them to remove the traces of juvenile occupancy from the lower part of the house.

In one way, this took some of the pressure off. The opening of the "hermit's" house to the friends of the "hermit's" housekeeper's fiancé and friends was a pleasant evidence of good will; people stopped wondering, a little.

On the other hand, James did not wholly approve. He contrasted this with what he remembered of his own home life. The guests who came to visit his mother and father were quiet and earnest. They indulged in animated discussions, argued points of deep reasoning, and in moments of relaxation they indulged in games that demanded skill and intellect.

Tim Fisher's friends were noisy and boisterous. They mixed highballs. They danced to music played so loud that it made the house throb. They watched the fights on television and argued with more volume than logic.

They were, to young James, a far cry from his parents' friends.

But, as he couldn't do anything about it, he refused to worry about it. James Holden turned his thoughts forward and began to plan how he was going to face the culmination of this romance next September Fifteenth. He even suspected that there would probably be a number of knotty little problems that he now knew nothing about; he resolved to allow some thinking-time to cope with them when, as, and if.

In the meantime, the summer was coming closer.

He prepared to make a visible show of having Mr. Charles Maxwell leave for a protracted summer travel. This would ease the growing problem of providing solid evidence of Maxwell's presence during the increasing frequency of Tim Fisher's visits and the widening circle of Mrs. Bagley's acquaintances in Shipmont. At the same time he and Martha would make a return from the Bolton School for Youth. This would allow them their freedom for the summer; for the first time James looked forward to it. Martha Bagley was progressing rapidly. This summer would see her over and done with the scatter-brain prattle that gave equal weight to fact or fancy. Her store of information was growing; she could be relied upon to maintain a fairly secure cover. Her logic was not to James Holden's complete satisfaction but she accepted most of his direction as necessary information to be acted upon now and reasoned later.

In the solving of his immediate problems, James can be forgiven for putting Paul Brennan out of his mind.

CHAPTER ELEVEN

But Paul Brennan was still alive, and he had not forgotten.

While James was, with astonishing success, building a life for himself in hiding, Brennan did everything he could to find him. That is to say, he did everything that—under the circumstances—he could afford to do.

The thing was, the boy had got clean away, without a trace.

When James escaped for the third, and very successful, time, Brennan was helpless. James had planned well. He had learned from his first two efforts. The first escape was a blind run toward a predictable objective; all right, that was a danger to be avoided. His second was entirely successful—until James created his own area of danger. Another lesson learned.

The third was planned with as much care as Napoleon's deliverance from the island.

James had started by choosing his time. He'd waited until Easter Week. He'd had a solid ten days during which he would be only one of countless thousands of children on the streets; there would be no slight suspicion because he was out when others were in.

James didn't go to school that day. That was common; children in the lower grades are often absent, and no one asks a question until they return, with the proper note from the parent. He was not missed anywhere until the school bus that should have dropped him off did not. This was an area of weakness that Brennan could not plug; he could hardly justify the effort of delivering and fetching the lad to and from school when the public school bus passed the Holden home. Brennan relied upon the Mitchells to see James upon the bus and to check him off when he returned. Whether James would have been missed earlier even with a personal delivery is problematical; certainly James would have had to concoct some other scheme to gain him his hours of free time.

At any rate, the first call to the school connected the Mitchells with a grumpy-voiced janitor who growled that teachers and principals had headed for their hills of freedom and wouldn't be back until Monday Week. It took some calling to locate a couple of James Holden's classmates who asserted that he hadn't been in school that day.

Paul Brennan knew at once what had happened, but he could not raise an immediate hue-and-cry. He fretted because of the Easter Week vacation; in any other time the sight of a school-aged boy free during school hours would have caused suspicion. During Easter Week vacation, every schoolboy would be free. James would also be protected by his size. A youngster walking alone is not suspect; his folks *must* be close by. The fact that it was "again" placed Paul Brennan in an undesirable position. This was not the youthful adventure that usually ends about three blocks from home. This was a repeat of the first absence during which James had been missing for months. People smile at the parents of the child who packs his little bag with a handkerchief and a candy bar to sally forth into the great big world, but it becomes another matter when the lad of six leaves home with every appearance of making it stick. So Brennan had to play it cozy, inviting newspaper reporters to the Holden home to display what he had to offer young James and giving them free rein to

question Brennan's housekeeper and general facto-
tum, the Mitchells. With honest-looking zeal, Paul
Brennan succeeded in building up a picture that de-
picted James as ungrateful, hard to understand, wilful,
and something of an intellectual brat.

Then the authorities proceeded to throw out a
fine-mesh dragnet. They questioned and cross-ques-
tioned bus drivers and railroad men. They made
contact with the local airport even though its facili-
ties were only used for a daisy-cutting feeder line. Pos-
ters were printed and sent to all truck lines for
display to the truck drivers. The roadside diners were
covered thoroughly. And knowing the boy's ability to
talk convincingly, the authorities even went so far as
to try the awesome project of making contact with
passengers bound out-of-town with young male children in tow.

Had James given them no previous experience to
think about, he would have been merely considered a
missing child and not a deliberate runaway. Then, instead of dragging down all of the known avenues of
standard escape, the townspeople would have organized a tree-by-tree search of the fields and woods
with hundreds of men walking hand in hand to inspect every square foot of the ground for either tracks
or the child himself. But the *modus operandi* of young
James Holden had been to apply sly touches such as
writing letters and forging signatures of adults to
cause the unquestioned sale of railroad tickets, or the
unauthorized ride in the side-door Pullman.

Therefore, while the authorities were extending
their circle of search based upon the velocity of modern transportation, James Holden was making his
slow way across field and stream, guided by a Boy
Scout compass and a U.S. Geodetic Survey map to
keep him well out of the reach of roadway or town.
With difficulty, but with dogged determination, he
carried a light cot-blanket into which he had rolled
four cans of pork and beans. He had a Boy Scout

knife and a small pair of pliers to open it with. He
had matches. He had the Boy Scout Handbook which
was doubly useful; the pages devoted to woodsman's
lore he kept for reference, the pages wasted on the
qualifications for merit badges he used to start fires.
He enjoyed sleeping in the open because it was
spring and pleasantly warm, and because the Boy
Scout Manual said that camping out was fun.

A grown man with an objective can cover thirty or
forty miles per day without tiring. James made it ten
to fifteen. Thus, by the time the organized search pe-
tered out for lack of evidence and manpower—try
asking one question of everybody within a hundred-
mile radius—James was quietly making his way, free
of care, like a hardy pioneer looking for a homestead
site.

The hint of kidnap went out early. The Federal
Bureau of Investigation, of course, could not move
until the waiting period was ended, but they did collect information and set up their organization ready
to move into high speed at the instant of legal time.
But then no ransom letter came; no evidence of the
crime of kidnaping. This did not close the case; there
were other cases on record where a child was stolen
by adults for purposes other than ransom. It was not
very likely that a child of six would be stolen by a
neurotic adult to replace a lost infant, and Paul Brennan was personally convinced that James Holden had
enough self-reliance to make such a kidnap attempt
fail rather early in the game. He could hardly say so,
nor could he suggest that James had indeed run away
deliberately and skilfully, and with planned steps
worthy of a much older person. He could only hint
and urge the F.B.I. into any action that he could coerce them into taking; he did not care how or who
brought James back just so long as the child was returned to his custody.

Then as the days wore into weeks with no sign, the

files were placed in the inactive drawer. Paul Brennan made contact with a few private agencies.

He was stopped here, again, by another angle. The Holdens were by no means wealthy. Brennan could not justify the offer of some reward so large that people simply could not turn down the slim chance of collecting. If the missing one is heir to a couple of million dollars, the trustees can justify a reward of a good many thousand dollars for his return. The amount that Brennan was prepared to offer could not compel the services of a private agency on a full-time basis. The best and the most interested of the agencies took the case on a contingent basis; if something turned their way in the due course of their work they'd immediately take steps. Solving the case of a complete disappearance on the part of a child who virtually vanished into thin air would be good advertising, but their advertising budget would not allow them to put one man on the case without the first shred of evidence to point the way.

If Paul Brennan had been aboveboard, he could have evoked a lot of interest. The search for a six-year-old boy with the educational development of a youth of about eighteen, informed through the services of an electromechanical device, would have fired public interest, Government intervention, and would also have justified Paul Brennan's depth of interest. But Paul Brennan could say nothing about the excellent training, he could only hint at James Holden's mental proficiency which was backed up by the boy's school record. As it was, Paul Brennan's most frightful nightmare was one where young James was spotted by some eagle-eyed detective and then in desperation—anything being better than an enforced return to Paul Brennan—James Holden pulled out all the stops and showed everybody precisely how well educated he really was.

In his own affairs, Paul still had to make a living, which took up his time. As guardian and trustee of the Holden Estate, he was responsible to the State for his handling of James Holden's inheritance. The State takes a sensible view of the disbursements of the inheritance of a minor. Reasonable sums may be spent on items hardly deemed necessities to the average person, but the ceiling called "reasonable" is a flexible term and subject to close scrutiny by the State.

In the long run it was Paul Brennan's own indefensible position that made it impossible to prosecute a proper search for the missing James Holden. Brennan suspected James of building up a bank account under some false name, but he could not saunter into banks and ask to examine their records without a Court order. Brennan knew that James had not taken off without preparation, but the examination of the stuff that James left behind was not very informative. There was a small blanket missing and Mrs. Mitchell said that it looked as though some cans had been removed from the stock but she could not be sure. And in a large collection of boy's stuff, one would not observe the absence of a Boy Scout knife and other trivia. Had a 100% inventory been available, the list of missing items would have pointed out James Holden's avenue of escape.

The search for an adult would have included questioning of banks. No one knows whether such a questioning would have uncovered the bank-by-mail routine conducted under the name of Charles Maxwell. It is not a regular thing, but the receipt of a check drawn on a New York bank, issued by a publishing company, and endorsed to be paid to the account of so-and-so, accompanied by a request to open an account in that name might never be connected with the manipulations of a six-year-old genius, who was overtly just plain bright.

And so Paul Brennan worried himself out of several pounds for fear that James would give himself away to the right people. He cursed the necessity of

keeping up his daily work routine. The hue-and-cry
he could not keep alive, but he knew that somewhere
there was a young boy entirely capable of reconstruct-
ing the whole machine that Paul Brennan wanted so
desperately that he had killed for it.

Paul Brennan was blocked cold. With the F.B.I.
maintaining a hands-off attitude because there was no
trace of any Federal crime involved, the case of James
Holden was relegated to the missing-persons files. It
became the official opinion that the lad had suffered
some mishap and that it would only be a matter of
time before his body was discovered. Paul Brennan
could hardly prove them wrong without explaining
the whole secret of James Holden's intelligence, competence, and the certainty that the young man would
improve upon both as soon as he succeeded in rebuilding the Holden Electromechanical Educator.

With the F.B.I. out of the picture, the local authorities waiting for the discovery of a small body, and the
state authorities shelving the case except for the
routine punch-card checks, official action died. Brennan's available reward money was not enough to buy
a private agency's interest full-time.

Brennan could not afford to tell anybody of his suspicion of James Holden's source of income, for the
idea of a child's making a living by writing would be
indefensible without full explanation. However, Paul
Brennan resorted to reading of magazines edited for
boys. Month after month he bought them and read
them, comparing the styles of the many writers against
the style of the manuscript copy left behind by James.

Brennan naturally assumed that James would use a
pen name. Writers often used pen names to conceal
their own identity for any one of several reasons. A
writer might use three or more pen names, each one
identified with a known style of writing, or a certain
subject or established character. But Paul Brennan
did not know all there was to know about the pen-
name business, such as an editor assigning a pen name

to prevent the too-often appearance of some prolific writer, or conversely to make one writer's name seem exclusive with his magazine; nor could Brennan know that a writer's literary standing can be kept high by assigning a pen name to any second-rate material he may be so unfortunate as to turn out.

Paul Brennan read many stories written by James Holden under several names, including the name of Charles Maxwell, but Brennan's identification according to literary style was no better than if he had tossed a coin.

And so, blocked by his own guilt and avarice from making use of the legal avenues of approach, Paul Brennan fumed and fretted away four long years while James Holden grew from six to ten years old, hiding under the guise of the Hermit of Martin's Hill and behind the pleasant adult façade of Mrs. Janet Bagley.

CHAPTER TWELVE

If Paul Brennan found himself blocked in his efforts to find James Holden and the re-created Holden Educator, James himself was annoyed by one evident fact: Everything he did resulted in spreading the news of the machine itself.

Had he been eighteen or so, he might have made out to his own taste. In the days of late teen-age, a youth can hold a job and rent a room, buy his own clothing and conduct himself to the limit of his ability. At ten he is suspect, because no one will permit him to paddle his own canoe. At a later age James could have rented a small apartment and built his machine alone. But starting as young as he did, he was forced to hide behind the cover of some adult, and he had picked Mrs. Bagley because he could control her both through her desire for security and the promise of a fine education for the daughter Martha Bagley.

The daughter was a two-way necessity; she provided him with a contemporary companion and also gave him a lever to wield against the adult. A lone woman could have made her way without trouble. A lone woman with a girl-child is up against a rather horrifying problem of providing both support and parental care. He felt that he had done what he had to do, up to the point where Mrs. Bagley became involved with Tim Fisher or anybody else. This part of adulthood was not yet within his grasp.

But there it was and here it is, and now there was

Martha to complicate the picture. Had Mrs. Bagley been alone, she and Tim could go off and marry and then settle down in Timbuctoo if they wanted to. But not with Martha. She was in the same intellectual kettle of sardines as James. Her taste in education was by no means the same. She took to the mathematical subjects indifferently, absorbing them well enough—once she could be talked into spending the couple of hours that each day demanded—but without interest. Martha could rattle off quotations from literary masters, she could follow the score of most operas (her voice was a bit off-key but she knew what was going on) and she enjoyed all of the available information on keeping a house in order. Her eye and her mind were, as James Holden's, faster than her hand. She went through the same frustrations as he did, with different tools and in a different medium. The first offside snick of the scissors she knew to be bad before she tried the pattern for size, and the only way she could correct such defective work was to practice and practice until her muscles were trained enough to respond to the direction of her mind.

Remove her now and place her in a school—even the most advanced school—and she would undergo the unhappy treatment that James had undergone these several years ago.

And yet she could not be cut loose. Martha was as much a part of this very strange life as James was. So this meant that any revision in overall policy must necessarily include the addition of Tim Fisher and not the subtraction of Mrs. Bagley and Martha.

"Charles Maxwell" had to go.

James's problem had not changed. His machine must be kept a secret as long as he could. The machine was his, James Quincy Holden's property by every known and unwritten legal right of direct, single, uncluttered inheritance. The work of his parents had been stopped by their death, but it was by no means finished with the construction of the machine. To the contrary, the real work had only begun with the completion of the first working model. And whether he turned out to be a machine-made genius, an over-powered dolt, or an introverted monster it was still his own personal reason for being alive.

He alone should reap the benefit or the sorrow, and had his parents lived they would have had their right to reap good or bad with him. Good or bad, had they lived, he would have received their protection.

As it was, he had no protection whatsoever. Until he could have and hold the right to control his own property as he himself saw fit, he had to hide just as deep from the enemy who would steal it as he must hide from the friend who would administrate it as a property in escrow for his own good, since he as a minor was legally unable to walk a path both fitting and proper for his feet.

So, the facts had to be concealed. Yet all he was buying was time.

By careful juggling, he had already bought some. Months with Jake Caslow, a few months stolidly fighting the school, and two with the help of Mrs. Bagley and Martha. Then in these later months there had been more purchased time; time gained by the postdated engagement and the procrastinated marriage, which was now running out.

No matter what he did, it seemed that the result was a wider spread of knowledge about the Holden Electromechanical Educator.

So with misgiving and yet unaware of any way or means to circumvent the necessity without doing more overall harm, James decided that Tim Fisher must be handed another piece of the secret. A plausible piece, with as much truth as he would accept for the time being. Maybe—hand Tim Fisher a bit with great gesture and he would not go prying for the whole?

His chance came in mid-August. It was after dinner on an evening uncluttered with party or shower or the horde of just-dropped-in-friends of whom Tim Fisher had legion.

Janet Bagley and Tim Fisher sat on the low divan in the living room half-facing each other. Apart, but just so far apart that they could touch with half a gesture, they were discussing the problem of domicile. They were also still quibbling mildly about the honeymoon. Tim Fisher wanted a short, noisy one. A ten-day stay in Hawaii, flying both ways, with a ten-hour stopover in Los Angeles on the way back. Janet Bagley wanted a long and lazy stay somewhere no closer than fifteen hundred miles to the nearest telephone, newspaper, mailbox, airline, bus stop, or highway. She'd take the 762-day rocket trip to Venus if they had one available. Tim was duly sympathetic to her desire to get away from her daily grind for as long a time as possible, but he also had a garage to run, and he was by no means incapable of pointing out the practical side of crass commercialism.

But unlike the problem of the honeymoon, which Janet Bagley was willing to discuss on any terms for the pleasure of discussing it, the problem of domicile had been avoided—to the degree of being pointed.

For Janet Bagley was still torn between two loyalties. Hers was not a lone loyalty to James Holden, there had been almost a complete association with the future of her daughter in the loyalty. She realized as well as James did, that Martha must not be wrested from this life and forced to live, forever an outcast, raised mentally above the level of her age and below the physical size of her mental development. Mrs. Bagley thought only of Martha's future; she gave little or no thought on the secondary part of the problem. But James knew that once Martha was separated from the establishment, she could not long conceal her advanced information, and revealing that would reveal its source.

And so, as they talked together with soft voices, James Holden decided that he could best buy time by employing logic, finance, and good common sense. He walked into the living room and sat across the coffee table from them. He said, "You'll have to live here, you know."

The abrupt statement stunned them both. Tim sat bolt upright and objected, "I'll see to it that we're properly housed, young fellow."

"This isn't charity," replied James. "Nor the goodness of my little heart. It's a necessity."

"How so?" demanded Tim crossly. "It's my life—and Janet's."

"And—Martha's life," added James.

"You don't think I'm including her out, do you?"

"No, but you're forgetting that she isn't to be popped here and there as the fancy hits you, either. She's much to be considered."

"I'll consider her," snapped Tim. "She shall be my daughter. If she will, I'll have her use my name as well as my care and affection."

"Of course you will," agreed James. The quick gesture of Mrs. Bagley's hand towards Tim, and his equally swift caress in reply were noticed but not understood by James. "But you're not thinking deeply enough about it."

"All right. You tell me all about it."

"Martha must stay here," said James. "Neither of you—nor Martha—have any idea of how stultifying it can be to be forced into school under the supervision of teachers who cannot understand, and among classmates whose grasp of any subject is no stronger than a feeble grope in the mental dawn."

"Maybe so. But that's no reason why we must run our life your way."

"You're wrong, Mr. Fisher. Think a moment. Without hesitation, you will include the education of Martha Bagley along with the 'care and affection' you mentioned a moment ago."

"Of course."

"This means, Mr. Fisher, that Martha, approaching ten years old, represents a responsibility of about seven more years prior to her graduation from high school and another four years of college—granting that Martha is a standard, normal, healthy young lady. Am I right?"

"Sure."

"Well, since you are happy and willing to take on the responsibility of eleven years of care and affection and the expense of schooling the girl, you might as well take advantage of the possibilities here and figure on five years—or less. If we cannot give her the equal of a master's degree in three, I'm shooting in the dark. Make it five, and she'll have her doctor's degree—or at least it's equivalent. Does that make sense?"

"Of course it does. But—"

"No buts until we're finished. You'll recall the tales we told you about the necessity of hiding out. It must continue. During the school year we must not be visible to the general public."

"But dammit, I don't want to set up my family in someone else's house," objected Tim Fisher.

"Buy this one," suggested James. "Then it will be yours. I'll stay on and pay rent on my section."

"You'll—now wait a minute! What are you talking about?"

"I said, '*I'll pay rent on my section*,'" said James.

"But this guy upstairs—" Tim took a long breath. "Let's get this straight," he said, "now that we're on the subject, what about Mr. Charles Maxwell?"

"I can best quote," said James with a smile, "'Oh, what a tangled web we weave, when first we practice to deceive!'"

"That's Shakespeare."

"Sorry. That's Sir Walter Scott. *The Lay of the Last Minstrel*. Canto Six, Stanza Seventeen. The fact of the matter is that we could go on compounding this lie, but it's time to stop it. Mr. Charles Maxwell does not exist."

"I don't understand!"

"Hasn't it puzzled you that this hermit-type character that never puts a foot out of the house has been out and gone on some unstated vacation or business trip for most of the spring and summer?"

"Hadn't given it a thought," said Fisher with a fatuous look at Mrs. Bagley. She mooned back at him. For a moment they were lost in one another, giving proof to the idea that blinder than he who will not see is the fellow who has his eye on a woman.

"Charles Maxwell does not exist except in the minds of his happy readers," said James. "He is a famous writer of boys' stories and known to a lot of people for that talent. Yet he is no more a real person than Lewis Carroll."

"But Lewis Carroll did exist—"

"As Charles L. Dodgson, a mathematician famous for his work in symbolic logic."

"All right! Then who writes these stories? Who supports you—and this house?"

"I do!"

Tim blinked, looked around the room a bit wildly and then settled on Martha, looking at her helplessly.

"It's true, Tim," she said quietly. "It's crazy but it works. I've been living with it for years."

Tim considered that for a full minute. "All right," he said shortly. "So it works. But why does any kid have to live for himself?" He eyed James. "Who's responsible for you?"

"I am!"

"But—"

"Got an hour?" asked James with a smile. "Then listen—"

At the end of James Holden's long explanation, Tim Fisher said, "Me—? Now, I need a drink!"

James chuckled, "Alcoholic, of course—which is Pi

to seven decimal places if you ever need it. Just count the letters."

Over his glass, Tim eyed James thoughtfully. "So if this is true, James, just who owns that fabulous machine of yours?"

"It is mine, or ours."

"You gave me to believe that it was a high-priority Government project," he said accusingly.

"Sorry. But I would lie as glibly to God Himself if it became necessary to protect myself by falsehood. I'm sorry it isn't a Government project, but it's just as important a secret."

"Anything as big as this *should* be the business of the Government."

"Perhaps so. But it's mine to keep or to give, and it's mine to study." James was thoughtful for a moment. "I suppose that you can argue that anything as important as this should be handed over to the authorities immediately; that a large group of men dedicated to such a study can locate its difficulties and its pitfalls and failures far swifter than a single youth of eleven. Yet by the right of invention, a process protected by the Constitution of the United States and circumvented by some very odd rulings on the part of the Supreme Court, it is mine by inheritance, to reap the exclusive rewards for my family's work. Until I'm of an age when I am deemed capable of managing my own life, I'd be 'protected' out of my rights if I handed this to anybody—including the Government. They'd start a commission full of bureaucrats who'd first use the machine to study how to best expand their own little empire, perpetuate themselves in office, and then they'd rule me out on the quaint theory that education is so important that it mustn't be wasted on the young."

Tim Fisher smiled wryly. He turned to Janet Bagley. "How do you want it?" he asked her.

"For Martha's sake, I want it his way," she said.

"All right. Then that's the way we'll have it," said

Tim Fisher. He eyed James somewhat ruefully. "You know, it's a funny thing. I've always thought this was a screwy setup, and to be honest, I've always thought you were a pretty bumptious kid. I guess you had a good reason. Anyway, I should have known Janet wouldn't have played along with it unless she had a reason that was really helping somebody."

James saw with relief that Tim had allied himself with the cause; he was, in fact, very glad to have someone knowledgeable and levelheaded in on the problem. Anyway he really liked Tim, and was happy to have the deception out of the way.

"That's all right," he said awkwardly.

Tim laughed. "Hey, will this contraption of yours teach me how to adjust a set of tappets?"

"No," said James quickly. "It will teach you the theory of how to chop down a tree but it can't show you how to swing an axe. Or," he went on with a smile, "it will teach you how to be an efficient accountant—but you have to use your own money!"

In the house on Martin's Hill, everybody won. Tim Fisher objected at first to the idea of gallivanting off on a protracted honeymoon, leaving a nine-year-old daughter in the care of a ten-year-old boy. But Janet—now Mrs. Fisher—pointed out that James and Martha were both quite competent, and furthermore there was little to be said for a honeymoon encumbered with a little pitcher that had such big ears, to say nothing of a pair of extremely curious eyes and a rather loud voice. And furthermore, if we allow the woman's privilege of adding one furthermore on top of another, it had been a long, long time since Janet had enjoyed a child-free vacation. So she won. It was not Hawaii by air for a ten-day stay. It was Hawaii by ship with a sixty-day sojourn in a hotel that offered both seclusion and company to the guests' immediate preference.

James Holden won more time. He felt that every

hour was a victory. At times he despaired because time passed so crawlingly slow. All the wealth of his education could not diminish that odd sense of the time-factor that convinces all people that the length of the years diminish as age increases. Far from being a simple, amusing remark, the problem has been studied because it is universal. It is psychological, of course, and it is not hard to explain simply in terms of human experience plus the known fact that the human senses respond to the logarithm of the stimulus.

With most people, time is reasonably important. We live by the clock, and we die by the clock, and before there were clocks there were candles marked in lengths and sand flowing through narrow orifices, water dripping into jars, and posts stuck in the ground with marks for the shadow to divide the day. The ancient ones related womanhood to the moon and understood that time was vital in the course of Life.

With James, time was more important, perhaps, than to any other human being alive. He was fighting for time, always. His was not the immature desire of uneducated youth to become adult overnight for vague reasons.

With James it was an honest evaluation of his precarious position. He had to hide until he was deemed capable of handling his own affairs, after which he could fight his own battles in his own way without the interference of the laws that are set up to protect the immature.

With Tim Fisher and his brand-new bride out of the way, James took a deep breath at having leaped one more hurdle. Then he sat down to think.

Obviously there is no great sea-change that takes place at the Stroke Of Midnight on the date of the person's 21st birthday; no magic wand is waved over his scalp to convert him in a moment of time from a puling infant to a mature adult. The growth of child to adult is as gradual as the increase of his stature, which varies from one child to the next.

The fact remained that few people are confronted by the necessity of making a decision based upon the precise age of the subject. We usually cross this barrier with no trouble, taking on our rights and responsibilities as we find them necessary to our life. Only in probating an estate left by the demise of both parents in the presence of minor children does this legal matter of precise age become noticeable. Even then, the control exerted over the minor by the legal guardian diminishes by some obscure mathematical proportion that approaches zero as the minor approaches the legal age of maturity. Rare is the case of the reluctant guardian who jealously relinquishes the iron rule only after the proper litigation directs him to let go, render the accounting for audit, and turn over the keys to the treasury to the rightful heir.

James Holden was the seldom case. James Holden needed a very adroit lawyer to tell him how and when his rights and privileges as a citizen could be granted, and under what circumstances. From the evidence already at hand, James saw loopholes available in the matter of the legal age of twenty-one. But he also knew that he could not approach a lawyer with questions without giving full explanation of every why and wherefor.

So James Holden, already quite competent in the do-it-himself method of cutting his own ice, decided to study law. Without any forewarning of the monumental proportions of the task he faced, James started to acquire books on legal procedure and the law.

With the return of Tim and Janet Fisher matters progressed well. Mrs. Fisher took over the running of the household; Tim continued his running of the garage and started to dicker for the purchase of the house on Martin's Hill. The "Hermit" who had returned before the wedding remained temporarily.

With a long-drawn plan, Charles Maxwell would slowly fade out of sight. Already his absence during the summer was hinting as being a medical study; during the winter he would return to the distant hospital. Later he would leave completely cured to take up residence elsewhere. Beyond this they planned to play it by ear.

James and Martha, freed from the housework routine, went deep into study.

Christmas passed and spring came and in April, James marked his eleventh birthday.

CHAPTER THIRTEEN

One important item continued to elude James Holden. The Educator could not be made to work in "tandem." In less technical terms, the Educator was strictly an individual device, a one-man-dog. The wave forms that could be recorded were as individual as fingerprints and pore-patterns and iris markings. James could record a series of ideas or a few pages of information and play them back to himself. During the playback he could think in no other terms; he could not even correct, edit or improve the phrasing. It came back word for word with the faithful reproduction of absolute fidelity. Similarly, Martha could record a phase of information and she, too, underwent the same repetition when her recording was played back to her.

But if Martha's recording were played through to James, utter confusion came. It was a whirling maze of colors and odors, sound, taste and touch.

It spoiled some of James Holden's hopes; he sought the way to mass-use, his plan was to employ a teacher to digest the information and then via the Educator, impress the information upon many other brains each coupled to the machine. This would not work.

He made an extra headset late in June and they tried it, sitting side-by-side and still it did not work. With Martha doing the reading, she got the full benefit of the machine and James emerged with a whirling head full of riotous colors and other sensations. At one point he hoped that they might learn some subject by sitting side-by-side and reading the text in unison, but from this they received the information horribly mingled with equal intensity of sensory noise.

He did not abandon this hope completely. He merely put it aside as a problem that he was not ready to study yet. He would re-open the question when he knew more about the whole process. To know the whole process meant studying many fields of knowledge and combining them into a research of his own.

And so James entered the summer months as he'd entered them before; Tim and Janet Fisher took off one day and returned the next afternoon with a great gay show of "bringing the children home for the summer."

Even in this day of multi-billion-dollar budgets and farm surpluses that cost forty thousand dollars per hour for warehouse rental, twenty-five hundred dollars is still a tidy sum to dangle before the eyes of any individual. This was the reward offered by Paul Brennan for any information as to the whereabouts of James Quincy Holden.

If Paul Brennan could have been honest, the information he could have supplied would have provided any of the better agencies with enough lead-material to track James Holden down in a time short enough to make the reward money worth the effort. Similarly, if James Holden's competence had been no greater than Brennan's scaled-down description, he could not have made his own way without being discovered.

Bound by his own guilt, Brennan could only fret. Everything including time, was running against him.

And as the years of James Holden's independence looked toward the sixth, Paul Brennan was willing to make a mental bet that the young man's education was deeper than ever.

He would have won. James was close to his dream

of making his play for an appearance in court and pleading for the law to recognize his competence to act as an adult. He abandoned all pretense; he no longer hid through the winter months, and he did not keep Martha under cover either. They went shopping with Mrs. Fisher now and then, and if any of the folks in Shipmont wondered about them, the fact that the children were in the care and keeping of responsible adults and were oh-so-quick on the uptake stopped anybody who might have made a fast call to the truant officer.

Then in the spring of James Holden's twelfth year and the sixth of his freedom, he said to Tim Fisher. "How would you like to collect twenty-five hundred dollars?"

Fisher grinned. "Who do you want killed?"

"Seriously."

"Who wouldn't?"

"All right, drop the word to Paul Brennan and collect the reward."

"Can you protect yourself?"

"I can quote Gladstone from one end to the other. I can cite every civil suit regarding the majority or minority problem that has any importance. If I fail, I'll skin out of there in a hurry on the next train. But I can't wait forever."

"What's the gimmick, James?"

"First, I am sick and tired of running and hiding, and I think I've got enough to prove my point and establish my rights. Second, there is a bit of cupidity here; the reward money is being offered out of my own inheritance so I feel that I should have some say in where it should go. Third, the fact that I steer it into the hands of someone I'd prefer to get it tickles my sense of humor. The trapper trapped; the bopper bopped; the sapper hoist by his own petard."

"And—?"

"It isn't fair to Martha, either. So the sooner we get

this whole affair settled, the sooner we can start to move towards a reasonable way of life."

"Okay, but how are we going to work it? I can't very well turn up by myself, you know."

"Why not?"

"People would think I'm a heel."

"Let them think so. They'll change their opinion once the whole truth is known." James smiled. "It'll also let you know who your true friends are."

"Okay. Twenty-five hundred bucks and a chance at the last laugh sounds good. I'll talk it over with Janet."

That night they buried Charles Maxwell, the Hermit of Martin's Hill.

BOOK THREE:
THE REBEL

CHAPTER FOURTEEN

In his years of searching, Paul Brennan had followed eleven fruitless leads. It had cost him over thirteen hundred dollars and he was prepared to go on and on until he located James Holden, no matter how much it took. He fretted under two fears, one that James had indeed suffered a mishap, and the other that James might reveal his secret in a dramatic announcement, or be discovered by some force or agency that would place the whole process in hands that Paul Brennan could not reach.

The registered letter from Tim Fisher culminated this six years of frantic search. Unlike the previous leads, this spoke with authority, named names, gave dates, and outlined sketchily but adequately the operations of the young man in very plausible prose. Then the letter went on in the manner of a man with his foot in a cleft stick; the writer did not approve of James Holden's operations since they involved his wife and newly-adopted daughter, but since wife and daughter were fond of James Holden, the writer could not make any overt move to rid his household of the interfering young man. Paul Brennan was asked to move with caution and in utter secrecy, even to sending the reward in cash to a special post-office box.

Paul Brennan's reaction was a disappointment to himself. He neither felt great relief nor the desire to exult. He found himself assaying his own calmness and wondering why he lacked emotion over this cul-

mination of so many years of futile effort. He re-read
the letter carefully to see if there were something hidden in the words that his subconscious had caught,
but he found nothing that gave him any reason to believe that this letter was a false lead. It rang true;
Brennan could understand Tim Fisher's stated reaction and the man's desire to collect. Brennan even
suspected that Fisher might use the reward money for
his own private purpose.

It was not until he read the letter for the third
time that he saw the suggestion to move with caution
and secrecy not as its stated request to protect the
writer, but as an excellent advice for his own
guidance.

And then Paul Brennan realized that for six years
he had been concentrating upon the single problem
of having James Holden returned to his custody, and
in that concentration he had lost sight of the more
important problem of achieving his true purpose of
gaining control of the Holden Educator. The letter
had not been the end of a long quest, but just the sig-
nal to start.

Paul Brennan of course did not give a fig for the
Holden Estate nor the welfare of James. His only interest was in the machine, and the secret of that
machine was locked in the young man's mind and
would stay that way unless James could be coerced
into revealing it. The secret indubitably existed as
hardware in the machine rebuilt in the house on
Martin's Hill, but Brennan guessed that any sight of
him would cause James to repeat his job of destruction. Brennan also envisioned a self-destructive device
that would addle the heart of the machine at the
touch of a button, perhaps booby-traps fitted like bur-
glar alarms that would ruin the machine at the first
touch of an untrained hand.

Brennan's mind began to work. He must plan his
moves carefully to acquire the machine by stealth. He
toyed with the idea of murder and rejected it as too

dangerous to chance a repeat, especially in view of the existence of the rebuilt machine.

Brennan read the letter again. It gave him to think. James had obviously succeeded in keeping his secret by imparting it to a few people that he could either trust or bind to him, perhaps with the offer of education via the machine, which James and only James maintained in hiding could provide. Brennan could not estimate the extent of James Holden's knowledge but it was obvious that he was capable of some extremely intelligent planning. He was willing to grant the boy the likelihood of being the equal of a long and experienced campaigner, and the fact that James was in the favor of Tim Fisher's wife and daughter meant that the lad would be able to call upon them for additional advice. Brennan counted the daughter Martha in this planning program, most certainly James would have given the girl an extensive education, too. Everything added up, even to Tim Fisher's resentment.

But there was not time to ponder over the efficiency of James Holden's operations. It was time for Paul Brennan to cope, and it seemed sensible to face the fact that Paul Brennan alone could not plot the illegal grab of the Holden Educator and at the same time masquerade as the deeply-concerned loving guardian. He could label James Holden's little group as an organization, and if he was to combat this organization he needed one himself.

Paul Brennan began to form a mental outline of his requirements. First he had to figure out the angle at which to make his attack. Once he knew the legal angle, then he could find ruthless men in the proper position of authority whose ambitions he could control. He regretted that the elder Holden had not allowed him to study civil and criminal law along with his courses in real estate and corporate law. As it was, Brennan was unsure of his legal rights, and he could not plan until he had researched the problem most thoroughly.

To his complete surprise, Paul Brennan discovered that there was no law that would stay an infant from picking up his marbles and leaving home. So long as the minor did not become a ward of responsibility of the State, his freedom was as inviolable as the freedom of any adult. The universal interest in missing-persons cases is overdrawn because of their dramatic appeal. In every case that comes to important notice, the missing person has left some important responsibilities that had to be satisfied. A person with no moral, legal, or ethical anchor has every right to pack his suitcase and catch the next conveyance for parts unknown. If he is found by the authorities after an appeal by friends or relatives, the missing party can tell the police that, Yes he did leave home and, No he isn't returning and, furthermore he does not wish his whereabouts made known; and all the authorities can report is that the missing one is hale, happy, and hearty and wants to stay missing.

Under the law, a minor is a minor and there is no proposition that divides one degree of minority from another. Major decisions, such as voting, the signing of binding contracts of importance, the determination of a course of drastic medical treatment, are deemed to be matters that require mature judgment. The age for such decisions is arbitrarily set at age twenty-one. Acts such as driving a car, sawing a plank, or buying food and clothing are considered to be "skills" that do not require judgment and therefore the age of demarkation varies with the state and the state legislature's attitude.

James was a minor; presumably he could repudiate contracts signed while a minor, at the time he reached the age of twenty-one. From a practical standpoint, however, anything that James contracted for was expendable and of vital necessity. He could not stop payment on a check for his rent, nor claim that he had not received proper payment for his stories and demand damages. Paul Brennan might possibly interfere with the smooth operation by squawking to the bank that Charles Maxwell was a phantom front for the minor child James Holden. And bankers, being bankers, might very well clog up the operation with a lot of questions. But there was the possibility that James Holden, operating through the agency of an adult, would switch his method. He could even go so far as to bring Brennan to lawsuit to have Brennan estopped fom his interference. Child or not, James Holden had been running a checking account by mail for a number of years which could be used as evidence of his good faith and ability.

Indeed, the position of James Holden was so solid that Brennan could only plead personal interest and personal responsibility in the case for securing a writ of habeas corpus to have the person of James Holden returned to his custody and protection. And this of itself was a bit on the dangerous side. A writ of habeus corpus will, by law, cause the delivery of the person to the right hands, but there is no part of the writ that can be used to guarantee that the person will remain thereafter. If Brennan tried to repeat this program, James Holden was very apt to suggest either the rather rare case of Barratry or Maintenance against Brennan. Barratry consists of the constant harassment of a citizen by the serial entry of lawsuit after lawsuit against him, each of which he must defend to the loss of time and money—and the tying up of courts and their officials. Maintenance is the reopening of the same suit and its charges time after time in court after court. One need only be sure of the attitude of the plantiff to strike back; if he is interested in heckling the defendant and this can be demonstrated in evidence, the heckler is a dead duck. Such a response would surely damage Paul Brennan's overt position as a responsible, interested, affectionate guardian of his best friends' orphaned child.

Then to put the top on the bottle, James Holden had crossed state lines in his flight from home. This meant that the case was not the simple proposition of appearing before a local magistrate and filing an emotional appeal. It was interstate. It smacked of extradition, and James Holden had committed no crime in either state.

To Paul Brennan's qualifications for his henchmen, he now added the need for flouting the law if the law could not be warped to fit his need.

Finding a man with ambition, with a casual disregard for ethics, is not hard in political circles. Paul Brennan found his man in Frank Manison, a rising figure in the office of the District Attorney. Manison had gubernatorial ambitions, and he was politically sharp. He personally conducted only those cases that would give him ironclad publicity; he preferred to lower the boom on a lighter charge than chance an acquittal. Manison also had a fine feeling for anticipating public trends, a sense of the drama, and an understanding of public opinion.

He granted Brennan a conference of ten minutes, and knowing from long experience that incoming information flows faster when it is not interrupted, he listened attentively, oiling and urging the flow by facial expressions of interest and by leaning forward attentively whenever a serious point was about to come forth. Brennan explained about James Holden, his superior education, and what it had enabled the lad to do. He explained the education not as a machine but as a "system of study" devised by James Holden's parents, feeling that it was better to leave a few stones lying flat and unturned for his own protection. Manison nodded at the end of the ten-minute time-limit, used his desk interphone to inform his secretary that he was not to be disturbed until further notice (which also told Paul Brennan that he was indeed interested) and then said:

"You know you haven't a legal leg to stand on, Brennan."

"So I find out. It seems incredible that there isn't any law set up to control the activity of a child."

"Incredible? No, Brennan, not so. To now it hasn't been necessary. People just do not see the necessity of laws passed to prevent something that isn't being done anyway. The number of outmoded laws, ridiculous laws, and laws passed in the heat of public emotion are always a subject for public ridicule. If the state legislature were to pass a law stating that any child under fourteen may not leave home without the consent of his parents, every opposition newspaper in the state would howl about the waste of time and money spent on ridiculous legislation passed to govern activities that are already under excellent control. They would poll the state and point out that for so many million children under age fourteen, precisely zero of them have left home to set up their own housekeeping. One might just as well waste the taxpayer's money by passing a law that confirms the Universal Law of Gravity.

"But that's neither here nor there," he said. "Your problem is to figure out some means of exerting the proper control over this intelligent infant."

"My problem rises higher than that," said Brennan ruefully. "He dislikes me to the point of blind, unreasonable hatred. He believes that I am the party responsible for the death of his parents and furthermore that the act was deliberate. Tantamount to a charge of first-degree murder."

"Has he made that statement recently?" asked Manison.

"I would hardly know."

"When last did you hear him say words to that effect?"

"At the time, following the accidental death of his

parents, James Holden ran off to the home of his grandparents. Puzzled and concerned, they called me as the child's guardian. I went there to bring him back to his home. I arrived the following morning and it was during that session that James Holden made the accusation."

"And he has not made it since, to the best of your knowledge?"

"Not that I know of."

"Hardly make anything out of that. Seven years ago. Not a formal charge, only a cry of rage, frustration, hysterical grief. The complaint of a five-year-old made under strain could hardly be considered slanderous. It is too bad that the child hasn't broken any laws. Your success in collecting him the first time was entirely due to the associations he'd made with this automobile thief—Caslow, you said his name was. We can't go back to that. The responsibility has been fixed, I presume, upon Jake Caslow in another state. Brennan, you've a real problem: How can you be sure that this James Holden will disclose his secret system of study even if we do succeed in cooking up some legal means of placing him and keep him in your custody?"

Brennan considered, and came to the conclusion that now was the time to let another snibbet of information go. "The system of study consists of an electronic device, the exact nature of which I do not understand. The entire machine is large and cumbersome. In it, as a sort of 'heart,' is a special circuit. Without this special circuit the thing is no more than an expensive aggregation of delicate devices that could be used elsewhere in electronics. One such machine stands unused in the Holden Home because the central circuit was destroyed beyond repair or replacement by young James Holden. He destroyed it because he felt that this secret should remain his own, the intellectual inheritance from his parents. There is one other machine—undoubtedly in full function and employed daily—in the house on Martin's Hill under James Holden's personal supervision."

"Indeed? How, may I ask?"

"It was rebuilt by James Holden from plans, specifications, and information engraved on his brain by his parents through the use of their first machine. Unfortunately, I have every reason to believe that this new machine is so booby-trapped and tamper-protected that the first interference by someone other than James Holden will cause its destruction."

"Um. It might be possible to impound this machine as a device of high interest to the State," mused Manison. "But if we start any proceeding as delicate as that, it will hit every newspaper in the country and our advantage will be lost."

"Technically," said Paul Brennan, "you don't know that such a machine exists. But as soon as young Holden realizes that you know about his machine, he'll also know that you got the information from me." Brennan sat quietly and thought for a moment. "There's another distressing angle, too," he said at last. "I don't think that there is a soul on earth who knows how to run this machine but James Holden. Steal it or impound it or take it away legally, you've got to know how it runs. I doubt that we'd find a half-dozen people on the earth who'd willingly sit in a chair with a heavy headset on, connected to a devilish aggregation of electrical machinery purported to educate the victim, while a number of fumblers experimented with the dials and the knobs and the switches. No sir, some sort of pressure must be brought to bear upon the youngster."

"Um. Perhaps civic pride? Might work. Point out to him that he is in control of a device that is essential to the security of the United States. That he is denying the children of this country the right to their extensive education. Et cetera?"

"Could be. But how are you going to swing it, technically in ignorance of the existence of such a machine?"

"Were I a member of the Congressional Committee on Education, I could investigate the matter of James Holden's apparent superiority of intellect."

"And hit Page One of every newspaper in the country," sneered Brennan.

"Well, I'm not," snapped Manison angrily. "However, there is a way, perhaps several ways, once we find the first entering wedge. After all, Brennan, the existence of a method of accelerating the course of educational training is of the utmost importance to the future of not only the United States of America, but the entire human race. Once I can locate some plausible reason for asking James Holden the first question about anything, the remainder of any session can be so slanted as to bring into the open any secret knowledge he may have. We, to make the disclosure easier, shall hold any sessions in the strictest of secrecy. We can quite readily agree with James Holden's concern over the long-range effectiveness of his machine and state that secrecy is necessary lest headstrong factions take the plunge into something that could be very detrimental to the human race instead of beneficial. Frankly, Mr. Brennan," said Manison with a wry smile, "I should like to borrow that device for about a week myself. It might help me locate some of the little legal points that would help me." He sighed. "Yes," he said sadly, "I know the law, but no one man knows all of the finer points. Lord knows," he went on, "if the law were a simple matter of behaving as it states, we'd not have this tremendous burden. But the law is subject to interpretation and change and argument and precedent— Precedent? Um, here we may have an interesting angle, Brennan. I must look into it."

"Precedent?"

"Yes, indeed. Any ruling that we were to make covering the right of a seven, eight, or nine year old to run his own life as he sees fit will be a ruling that establishes precedent."

"And—?"

"Well, up to now there's no ruling about such a case; no child of ten has ever left home to live as he prefers. But this James Holden is apparently capable of doing just that—and any impartial judge deliberating such a case would find it difficult to justify a decision that placed the competent infant under the guardianship and protection of an adult who is less competent than the infant."

Brennan's face turned dark. "You're saying that this Holden kid is smarter than I am?"

"Sit down and stop sputtering," snapped Manison. "What were you doing at six years old, Brennan? Did you have the brains to leave home and protect yourself by cooking up the plausible front of a very interesting character such as the mythical Hermit of Martin's Hill? Were you writing boys' stories for a nationwide magazine of high circulation and accredited quality? Could you have planned your own dinner and prepared it, or would you have dined on chocolate bars washed down with strawberry pop? Stop acting indignant. Start thinking. If for no other reason than that we don't want to end up selling pencils on Halstead Street because we're not quite bright, we've got to lay our hands on that machine. We've got to lead, not follow. Yet at the present time I'll wager that your James Holden is going to give everybody concerned a very rough time. Now, let me figure out the angles and pull the wires. One thing that nobody can learn from any electronic machine is how to manipulate the component people that comprise a political machine. I'll be in touch with you, Brennan."

The ring at the door was Chief of Police Joseph Colling and another gentleman. Janet Fisher answered the door, "Good evening, Mr. Colling. Come in?"

"Thank you," said Colling politely. "This is Mr. Frank Manison, from the office of the State Department of Justice."

"Oh? Is something wrong?"

"Not that we know of," replied Manison. "We're simply after some information. I apologize for calling at eight o'clock in the evening, but I wanted to catch you all under one roof. Is Mr. Fisher home? And the children?"

"Why, yes. We're all here." Janet stepped aside to let them enter the living room, and then called upstairs. Mr. Manison was introduced around and Tim Fisher said, cautiously, "What's the trouble here?"

"No trouble that we know of," said Manison affably. "We're just after some information about the education of James Holden, a legal minor, who seems never to have been enrolled in any school."

"If you don't mind," replied Tim Fisher, "I'll not answer anything without the advice of my attorney."

Janet Fisher gasped.

Tim turned with a smile. "Don't you like lawyers, honey?"

"It isn't that. But isn't crying for a lawyer an admission of some sort?"

"Sure is," replied Tim Fisher. "It's an admission that I don't know all of my legal rights. If lawyers come to me because they don't know all there is to know about the guts of an automobile, I have every right to the same sort of consultation in reverse. Agree, James?"

James Holden nodded. "The man who represents himself in court has a fool for a client," he said. "I think that's Daniel Webster, but I'm not certain. No matter; it's right. Call Mr. Waterman, and until he arrives we'll discuss the weather, the latest dope in high-altitude research, or nuclear physics."

Frank Manison eyed the lad. "You're James Holden?"

"I am."

Tim interrupted. "We're not answering *anything*," he warned.

"Oh, I don't mind admitting my identity," said James. "I've committed no crime, I've broken no law. No one can point to a single act of mine that shows a shred of evidence to the effect that my intentions are not honorable. Sooner or later this whole affair had to come to a showdown, and I'm prepared to face it squarely."

"Thank you," said Manison. "Now, without inviting comment, let me explain one important fact. The state reserves the right to record marriages, births, and deaths as a simple matter of vital statistics. We feel that we have every right to the compiling of the census, and we can justify our feeling. I am here because of some apparent irregularities, records of which we do not have. If these apparent irregularities can be explained to our satisfaction for the record, this meeting will be ended. Now, let's relax until your attorney arrives."

"May I get you some coffee or a highball?" asked Janet Fisher.

"Coffee, please," agreed Frank Manison. Chief Colling nodded quietly. They relaxed over coffee and small talk for a half hour. The arrival of Waterman, Tim Fisher's attorney, signalled the opening of the discussion.

"First," said Manison, his pencil poised over a notebook, "Who lives here in permanent residence, and for how long?" He wrote rapidly as they told him. "The house is your property?" he asked Tim, and wrote again. "And you are paying a rental on certain rooms of this house?" he asked James, who nodded.

"Where did you attend school?" he asked James.

"I did not."

"Where did you get your education?"

"By a special course in home study."

"You understand that under the state laws that provide for the education of minor children, the curriculum must be approved by the state?"

"I do."

"And has it?"

Waterman interrupted. "Just a moment, Mr. Manison. In what way must the curriculum be approved? Does the State study all textbooks and the manner in which each and every school presents them? Or does the State merely insist that the school child be taught certain subjects?"

"The State merely insists that certain standards of education be observed."

"In fact," added James, "the State does not even insist that the child *learn* the subjects, realizing that some children lack the intellect to be taught certain subjects completely and fully. Let's rather say that the State demands that school children be exposed to certain subjects in the hope that they 'take.' Am I not correct?"

"I presume you are."

"Then I shall answer your question. In my home study, I have indeed followed the approved curriculum by making use of the approved textbooks in their proper order. I am aware of the fact that this is not the same State, but if you will consult the record of my earlier years in attendance at a school selected by my legal guardian, you'll find that I passed from preschool grade to Fourth Grade in a matter of less than half a year, at the age of five-approaching-six. If this matter is subject to question, I'll submit to any course of extensive examination your educators care to prepare. The law regarding compulsory education in this state says that the minor child must attend school until either the age of eighteen, or until he has completed the standard eight years of grammar school and four years of high school. I shall then stipulate that the suggested examination be limited to the schooling of a high school graduate."

"For the moment we'll pass this over. We may ask that you do prove your contention," said Manison.

"You don't doubt that I can, do you?" asked James.

Manison shook his head. "No, at this moment I have no doubt."

"Then why do you bother asking?"

"I am here for a rather odd reason," said Manison. "I've told you the reservations that the State holds, which justify my presence. Now, it is patently obvious that you are a very competent young man, James Holden. The matter of making your own way is difficult, as many adults can testify. To have contrived a means of covering up your youth, in addition to living a full and competent life, demonstrates an ability above and beyond the average. Now, the State is naturally interested in anything that smacks of acceleration of the educational period. Can you understand that?"

"Naturally. None but a dolt would avoid education."

"Then you agree with our interest?"

"I—"

"Just a moment, James," said Waterman. "Let's put it that you understand their interest, but that you do not necessarily agree."

"I understand," said James.

"Then you must also understand that this 'course of study' by which you claim the equal of a high-school education at the age of ten or eleven (perhaps earlier) must be of high importance."

"I understand that it might," agreed James.

"Then will you explain why you have kept this a secret?"

"Because—"

"Just a moment," said Waterman again. "James, would you say that your method of educating yourself is completely perfected?"

"Not completely."

"Not perfected?" asked Manison. "Yet you claim to have the education of a high-school graduate?"

"I so claim," said James. "But I must also point out that I have acquired a lot of mish-mash in the course of this education. For instance, it is one thing to study English, its composition, spelling, vocabulary, construction, rules and regulations. One must learn these things if he is to be considered literate. In the course of such study, one also becomes acquainted with English literature. With literature it is enough to merely be acquainted with the subject. One need not know the works of Chaucer or Spenser intimately—unless one is preparing to specialize in the English literature of the writers of that era. Frankly, sir, I should hate to have my speech colored by the flowery phrases of that time, and the spelling of that day would flunk me out of First Grade if I made use of it. In simple words, I am still perfecting the method."

"Now, James," went on Waterman, "have you ever entertained the idea of not releasing the details of your method?"

"Occasionally," admitted James.

"Why?"

"Until we know everything about it, we can not be certain that its ultimate effect will be wholly beneficial."

"So, you see," said Waterman to Manison, "the intention is reasonable. Furthermore, we must point out that this system is indeed the invention created by the labor and study of the parents of James Holden, and as such it is a valuable property retained by James Holden as his own by the right of inheritance. The patent laws of the United States are clear, it is the many conflicting rulings that have weakened the system. The law itself is contained in the Constitution of the United States, which provides for the establishment of a Patent Office as a means to encourage inventors by granting them the exclusive right to the benefits of their labor for a reasonable period of time—namely seventeen years with provision for a second period under renewal."

"Then why doesn't he make use of it?" demanded Manison.

"Because the process, like so many another process, can be copied and used by individuals without payment, and because there hasn't been a patent suit upheld for about forty years, with the possible exception of Major Armstrong's suit against the Radio Corporation of America, settled in Armstrong's favor after about twenty-five years of expensive litigation. A secret is no longer a secret these days, once it has been written on a piece of paper and called to the attention of a few million people across the country."

"You realize that anything that will give an extensive education at an early age is vital to the security of the country."

"We recognize that responsibility, sir," said Waterman quietly. "We also recognize that in the hands of unscrupulous men, the system could be misused. We also realize its dangers, and we are trying to avoid them before we make the announcement. We are very much aware of the important, although unfortunate, fact that James Holden, as a minor, can have his rights abridged. Normally honest men, interested in the protection of youth, could easily prevent him from using his own methods, thus depriving him of the benefits that are legally his. This could be done under the guise of protection, and the result would be the super-education of the protectors—whose improving intellectual competence would only teach them more and better reasons for depriving the young man of his rights. James Holden has a secret, and he has a right to keep that secret, and his only protection is for him to continue to keep that secret inviolate. It was his parents' determination not to release this process upon the world until they were certain of the results. James is a living example of their effort; they conceived him for the express purpose of providing a virgin mind to educate by their methods, so that no outside interference would becloud their results. If this can be construed as the illegal experimentation on animals under the anti-vivisection laws, or cruelty to children, it was their act, not his. Is that clear?"

"It is clear," replied Manison. "We may be back for more discussion on this point. I'm really after information, not conducting a case, you know."

"Well, you have your information."

"Not entirely. We've another point to consider, Mr. Waterman. It is admittedly a delicate point. It is the matter of legal precedent. Granting everything you say is true—and I'll grant that hypothetically for the purpose of this argument—let's assume that James Holden ultimately finds his process suitable for public use. Now, happily to this date James had not broken any laws. He is an honorable individual. Let's now suppose that in the near future, someone becomes educated by his process and at the age of twelve or so decided to make use of his advanced intelligence in nefarious work?"

"All right. Let's suppose."

"Then you tell me who is responsible for the person of James Holden?"

"He is responsible unto himself."

"Not under the existing laws," said Manison. "Let's consider James just as we know him now. Who says, 'go ahead,' if he has an attack of acute appendicitis?"

"In the absence of someone to take the personal responsibility," said James quietly, "the attending doctor would toss his coin to see whether his Oath of Hippocrates was stronger than his fear of legal reprisals. It's been done before. But let's get to the point, Mr. Manison. What do you have in mind?"

"You've rather pointedly demonstrated your preference to live here rather than with your legally-appointed guardian."

"Yes."

"Well, young man, I suggest that we get this matter settled legally. You are not living under the supervision of your guardian, but you are indeed living under the auspices of people who are not recognized by law as holding the responsibility for you."

"So far there's been no cause for complaint."

"Let's keep it that way," smiled Manison. "I'll ask you to accept a writ of habeas corpus, directing you to show just cause why you should not be returned to the custody of your guardian."

"And what good will that do?"

"If you can show just cause," said Manison, "the Court will follow established precedent and appoint Mr. and Mrs. Fisher as your responsible legal guardians—if that is your desire."

"Can this be done?" asked Mrs. Fisher.

"It's been done before, time and again. The State is concerned primarily with the welfare of the child; children have been legally removed from natural but unsuitable parents, you know." He looked distressed for a moment and then went on, "The will of the deceased is respected, but the law recognizes that it is the living with which it must be primarily concerned, that mistakes can be made, and that such errors in judgment must be rectified in the name of the public weal."

"I've been—" started James but Attorney Waterman interrupted him:

"We'll accept the service of your writ, Mr. Manison." And to James after the man had departed: "Never give the opposition an inkling of what you have in mind—and always treat anybody who is not in your retainer as opposition."

CHAPTER FIFTEEN

The case of Brennan vs Holden opened in the emptied court room of Judge Norman L. Carter, with a couple of bored members of the press wishing they were elsewhere. For the first two hours, it was no more than formalized outlining of the whole situation.

The plaintiff identified himself, testified that he was indeed the legal guardian of the minor James Quincy Holden, entered a transcript of the will in evidence, and then went on to make his case. He had provided a home atmosphere that was, to the best of his knowledge, the type of home atmosphere that would have been highly pleasing to the deceased parents—especially in view of the fact that this home was one and the same house as theirs and that little had been changed. He was supported by the Mitchells. It all went off in the slow, cumbersome dry phraseology of the legal profession and the sum and substance of two hours of back-and-forth question-and-answer was to establish the fact that Paul Brennan had provided a suitable home for the minor, James Quincy Holden, and that the minor James Quincy Holden had refused to live in it and had indeed demonstrated his objections by repeatedly absenting himself wilfully and with premeditation.

The next half hour covered a blow-by-blow account of Paul Brennan's efforts to have the minor restored to him. The attorneys for both sides were alert. Brennan's counsel did not even object when Waterman paved the way to show why James Holden wanted his freedom by asking Brennan:

"Were you aware that James Holden was a child of exceptional intellect?"

"Yes."

"And you've testified that when you moved into the Holden home, you found things as the Holdens had provided them for their child?"

"Yes."

"In your opinion, were these surroundings suitable for James Holden?"

"They were far too advanced for a child of five."

"I asked specifically about James Holden."

"James Holden was five years old."

Waterman eyed Brennan with some surprise, then cast a glance at Frank Manison, who sat at ease, calmly watching and listening with no sign of objection. Waterman turned back to Brennan and said, "Let's take one more turn around Robin Hood's Barn, Mr. Brennan. First, James Holden was an exceptional child?"

"Yes."

"And the nature of his toys and furnishings?"

"In my opinion, too advanced for a child of five."

"But were they suitable for James Holden?"

"James Holden was a child of five."

Waterman faced Judge Carter. "Your Honor," he said, "I submit that the witness is evasive. Will you direct him to respond to my direct question with a direct answer?"

"The witness will answer the question properly," said Judge Carter with a slight frown of puzzlement, "unless counsel for the witness has some plausible objection?"

"No objection," said Manison.

"Please repeat or rephrase your question," suggested Judge Carter.

"Mr. Brennan," said Waterman, "you've testified that James was an exceptional child, advanced beyond his years. You've testified that the home and surroundings provided by James Holden's parents reflected this fact. Now tell me, were the toys, surroundings, and the home suitable for James Holden?"

"In my opinion, no."

"And subsequently you replaced them with stuff you believed more suitable for a child of five, is that it?"

"Yes. I did, and you are correct."

"To which he objected?"

"To which James Holden objected."

"And what was your reponse to his objection?"

"I overruled his objection."

"Upon what grounds?"

"Upon the grounds that the education and the experience of an adult carries more wisdom than the desires of a child."

"Now, Mr. Brennan, please listen carefully. During the months following your guardianship, you successively removed the books that James Holden was fond of reading, replaced his advanced Meccano set with a set of modular blocks, exchanged his oil-painting equipment for a child's coloring books and standard crayolas, and in general you removed everything interesting to a child with known superiority of intellect?"

"I did."

"And your purpose in opening this hearing was to convince this Court that James Holden should be returned by legal procedure to such surroundings?"

"It is."

"No more questions," said Waterman. He sat down and rubbed his forehead with the palm of his right hand, trying to think.

Manison said, "I have one question to ask of Janet Fisher, known formerly as Mrs. Bagley."

Janet Fisher was sworn and properly identified.

"Now, Mrs. Fisher, prior to your marriage to Mr. Fisher and during your sojourn with James Holden in the House on Martin's Hill, did you supervise the activities of James Holden?"

"No," she said.

"Thank you," said Manison. He turned to Waterman and waved him to any cross-questioning.

Still puzzled, Waterman asked, "Mrs. Fisher, who did supervise the House on Martin's Hill?"

"James Holden."

"During those years, Mrs. Fisher, did James Holden at any time conduct himself in any other manner but the actions of an honest citizen? I mean, did he perform or suggest the performance of any illegal act to your knowledge?"

"No, he did not."

Waterman turned to Judge Carter. "Your Honor," he said, "it seems quite apparent to me that the plaintiff in this case has given more testimony to support the contentions of my client than they have to support their own case. Will the Court honor a petition that the case be dismissed?"

Judge Norman L. Carter smiled slightly. "This is irregular," he said. "You should wait for that petition until the plaintiff's counsel has closed his case, you know." He looked at Frank Manison. "Any objection?"

Manison said, "Your Honor, I have permitted my client to be shown in this questionable light for no other purpose than to bring out the fact that any man can make a mistake in the eyes of other men when in reality he was doing precisely what he thought to be the best thing to do for himself and for the people within his responsibility. The man who raises his child to be a roustabout is wrong in the eyes of his neighbor who is raising his child to be a scientist, and vice versa. We'll accept the fact that James Holden's mind is superior. We'll point out that there have been many cases of precocious children or child geniuses who make a strong mark in their early years and drop into oblivion by the time they're twenty.

Now, consider James Holden, sitting there discussing something with his attorney. I have no doubt in the world that he could conjugate Latin verbs, discuss the effect of the Fall of Rome on Western Civilization, and probably compute the orbit of an artificial satellite. But can James Holden fly a kite or shoot a marble? Has he ever had the fun of sliding into third base, or whittling on a peg, or any of the other enjoyable trivia of boyhood? Has he—"

"One moment," said Judge Carter. "Let's not have an impassioned oration, counsel. What is your point?"

"James Holden has a legal guardian, appointed by law at the express will of his parents. Headstrong, he has seen fit to leave that protection. He is fighting now to remain away from that protection. I can presume that James Holden would prefer to remain in the company of the Fishers where, according to Mrs. Fisher, he was not responsible to her whatsoever, but rather ran the show himself. I—"

"You can't make that presumption," said Judge Carter. "Strike it from the record."

"I apologize," said Manison. "But I object to dismissing this case until we find out just what James Holden has in mind for his future."

"I'll hold Counsel Waterman's petition in abeyance until the point you mention is in the record," said Judge Carter. "Counsel, are you finished?"

"Yes," said Manison. "I'll rest."

"Mr. Waterman?"

Waterman said, "Your Honor, we've been directed to show just cause why James Holden should not be returned to the protection of his legal guardian. Counsel has implied that James Holden desires to be placed in the legal custody of Mr. and Mrs. Fisher. This is a pardonable error whether it stands in the record or not. The fact is that James Holden does not need protection, nor does he want protection. To the contrary, James Holden petitions this Court to declare him legally competent so that he may conduct his own affairs with the rights, privileges, and indeed, even the *risks* taken by the status of adult.

"I'll point out that the rules and laws that govern the control and protection of minor children were passed by benevolent legislators to prevent exploitation, cruelty, and deprivation of the child's life by men who would take advantage of his immaturity. However we have here a young man of twelve who has shown his competence to deal with the adult world by actual practice. Therefore it is our contention that protective laws are not only unnecessary, but undesirable because they restrict the individual from his desire to live a full and fruitful life.

"To prove our contention beyond any doubt, I'll ask that James Holden be sworn in as my first witness."

Frank Manison said, "I object, Your Honor. James Holden is a minor and not qualified under law to give creditable testimony as a witness."

Waterman turned upon Manison angrily. "You really mean that you object to my case *per se*."

"That, too," replied Manison easily.

"Your Honor, I take exception! It is my purpose to place James Holden on the witness stand, and there to show this Court and all the world that he is of honorable mind, properly prepared to assume the rights of an adult. We not only propose to show that he acted honorably, we shall show that James Holden consulted the law to be sure that whatever he did was not illegal."

"Or," added Manison, "was it so that he would know how close to the limit he could go without stepping over the line?"

"Your Honor," asked Waterman, "can't we have your indulgence?"

"I object! The child is a minor."

"I accept the statement!" stormed Waterman. "And

I say that we intend to prove that this minor is qualified to act as an adult."

"And," sneered Manison, "I'll guess that one of your later arguments will be that Judge Carter, having accepted this minor as qualified to deliver sworn testimony, has already granted the first premise of your argument."

"I say that James Holden has indeed shown his competence already by actually doing it!"

"While hiding under a false façade!"

"A façade forced upon him by the restrictive laws that he is petitioning the Court to set aside in his case so that he need hide no longer."

Frank Manison said, "Your Honor, how shall the case of James Holden be determined for the next eight or ten years if we do grant James Holden this legal right to conduct his own affairs as an adult? That we must abridge the laws regarding compulsory education is evident. James Holden is twelve years and five months old. Shall he be granted the right to enter a tavern to buy a drink? Will his request for a license to marry be honored? May he enter the polling place and cast his vote? The contention of counsel that the creation of Charles Maxwell was a physical necessity is acceptable. But what happens without 'Maxwell'? Must we prepare a card of identity for James Holden, stating his legal status, and renew it every year like an automobile license because the youth will grow in stature, add to his weight, and ultimately grow a beard? Must we enter on this identification card the fact that he is legally competent to sign contracts, rent a house, write checks, and make his own decision about the course of dangerous medical treatment—or shall we list those items that he is not permitted to do such as drinking in a public place, cast his vote, or marry? This State permits a youth to drive an automobile at the age of sixteen, this act being considered a skill rather than an act that requires judgment. Shall James Holden be permitted to drive an automobile even though he can not reach the foot pedals from any position where he can see through the windshield?"

Judge Carter sat quietly. He said calmly, "Let the record show that I recognize the irregularity of this procedure and that I permit it only because of the unique aspects of this case. Were there a Jury, I would dismiss them until this verbal exchange of views and personalities has subsided.

"Now," he went on, "I will not allow James Holden to take the witness stand as a qualified witness to prove that he is a qualified witness. I am sure that he can display his own competence with a flow of academic brilliance, or his attorney would not have tried to place him upon the stand where such a display could have been demonstrated. Of more importance to the Court and to the State is an equitable disposition of the responsibility to and over James Quincy Holden."

Judge Norman L. Carter leaned forward and looked from Frank Manison to James Holden, and then to Attorney Waterman.

"We must face some awkward facts," he said. "If I rule that he be returned to Mr. Brennan, he will probably remain no longer than he finds it convenient, at which point he will behave just as if this Court had never convened. Am I not correct, Mr. Manison?"

"Your Honor, you are correct. However, as a member of the Department of Justice of this State, I suggest that you place the responsibility in my hands. As an Officer of the Court, my interest would be to the best interest of the State rather than based upon experience, choice, or opinion as to what is better for a five-year-old or a child prodigy. In other words, I would exert the control that the young man needed. At the same time I would not make the mistakes that were made by Mr. Brennan's personal opinion of how a child should be reared."

Waterman shouted, "I object, Your Honor. I object—"

Brennan leaped to his feet and cried, "Manison, you can't freeze me out—"

James Holden shrilled, "I won't! I won't!"

Judge Carter eyed them one by one, staring them into silence. Finally he looked at Janet Fisher and said, "May I also presume that you would be happy to resume your association with James Holden?"

She nodded and said, "I'd be glad to," in a sincere voice. Tim Fisher nodded his agreement.

Brennan whirled upon them and snarled. "My reward money—" but he was shoved down in his seat with a heavy hand by Frank Manison who snapped, "Your money bought what it was offered for. So now shut up, you utter imbecile!"

Judge Norman L. Carter cleared his throat and said, "This great concern over the welfare of James Holden is touching. We have Mr. Brennan already twice a loser and yet willing to try it for three times. We have Mr. and Mrs. Fisher who are not dismayed at the possibility of having their home occupied by a headstrong youth whose actions they cannot control. We find one of the ambitious members of the District Attorney's Office offering to take on an additional responsibility—all, of course, in the name of the State and the welfare of James Holden, Finally we have James Holden who wants no part of the word 'protection' and claims the ability to run his own life.

"Now it strikes me that assigning the responsibility for this young man's welfare is by no means the reason why you all are present, and it similarly occurs to me that the young man's welfare is of considerably less importance than the very interesting question of how and why this young man has achieved so much."

With a thoughtful expression, Judge Carter said, "James Holden, how did you acquire this magnificent education at the tender age of twelve-plus?"

"I—"

"I object!" cried Frank Manison. "The minor is not qualified to give testimony."

"Objection overruled. This is not testimony. I have every right in the world to seek out as much information from whatever source I may select; and I have the additional right to inspect the information I receive to pass upon its competence and relevance. Sit down, counsel!"

Manison sat grumpily and Judge Carter eyed James again, and James took a full breath. This was the moment he had been waiting for.

"Go on, James. Answer my question. Where did you come by your knowledge?"

James Holden stood up. This was the question that had to arise; he was only surprised it had taken so long.

He said calmly: "Your Honor, you may not ask that question."

"I may not?" asked Judge Carter with a lift of his eyebrows.

"No sir. You may not."

"And just why may I not?"

"If this were a criminal case, and if you could establish that some of my knowledge were guilty knowledge, you could then demand that I reveal the source of my guilty knowledge and under what circumstance it was obtained. If I refused to disclose my source, I could then be held in contempt of court or charged with being an accessory to the corpus of the crime. However, this is a court hearing to establish whether or not I am competent under law to manage my own affairs. How I achieve my mental competence is not under question. Let us say that it is a process that is my secret by the right of inheritance from my parents and as such it is valuable to me so long as I can demand payment for its use."

"This information may have a bearing on my ruling."

"Your Honor, the acquisition of knowledge or information *per se* is concomitant with growing up. I can and will demonstrate that I have the equivalent of the schooling necessary to satisfy both this Court and the State Board of Education. I will state that my education has been acquired by concentration and application in home study, and that I admit to attendance at no school. I will provide you or anybody else with a list of the books from which I have gleaned my education. But whether I practice Yoga, Dianetics, or write the lines on a sugarcoated pill and swallow it is my trade secret. It can not be extracted from me by any process of the law because no illegality exists."

"And what if I rule that you are not competent under the law, or withhold judgment until I have had an opportunity to investigate these ways and means of acquiring an accelerated education?"

"I'll then go on record as asking you to disbar yourself from this hearing on the grounds that you are not an impartial judge of the justice in my case."

"Upon what grounds?"

"Upon the grounds that you are personally interested in being provided with a process whereby you may acquire an advanced education yourself."

The judge looked at James thoughtfully for a moment. "And if I point out that any such process is of extreme interest to the State and to the Union itself, and as such must be disclosed?"

"Then I shall point out that your ruling is based upon a personal opinion because you don't know anything about the process. If I am ruled a legal minor you cannot punish me for not telling you my secrets, and if I am ruled legally competent, I am entitled to my own decision."

"You are within your rights," admitted Judge Carter with some interest. "I shall not make such a demand. But I now ask you if this process of yours is both safe and simple."

...roperly used with some good judgment."

"...ow listen to me carefully," said Judge Carter. "Is it not true that your difficulties in school, your inability to get along with your classmates, and your having to hide while you toiled for your livelihood in secret—these are due to this extensive education brought about through your secret process?"

"I must agree, but—"

"You must agree," interrupted Judge Carter. "Yet knowing these unpleasant things did not deter you from placing, or trying to place, the daughter of your housekeeper in the same unhappy state. In other words, you hoped to make an intellectual misfit out of her, too?"

"I—now see here—"

"You see here! Did you or did you not aid in the education of Martha Bagley, now Martha Fisher?"

"Yes, I did, and—"

"Was that good judgment, James Holden?"

"What's wrong with higher education?" demanded James angrily.

"Nothing, if it's acquired properly."

"But—"

"Now listen again. If I were to rule in your favor, would Martha Fisher be the next bratling in a long and everlasting line of infant supermen applying to this and that and the other Court to have their legal majority ruled, each of them pointing to your case as having established precedence?"

"I have no way of predicting the future, sir. What may happen in the future really has no bearing in evidence here."

"Granted that it does not. But I am not going to establish a dangerous precedent that will end with doctors qualified to practice surgery before they are big enough to swing a stethoscope or attorneys that plead a case before they are out of short pants. I am going to recess this case indefinitely with a partial ruling. First, until this process of yours comes under official study, I am declaring you, James Holden, to be a Ward of this State, under the jurisdiction of this Court. You will have the legal competence to act in matters of skill, including the signing of documents and instruments necessary to your continued good health. In all matters that require mature judgment, you will report to this Court and all such questions shall be rendered after proper deliberation either in open session or in chambers, depending upon the Court's opinion of their importance. The court stenographer will now strike all of the testimony given by James Holden from the record."

"I object!" exploded Brennan's attorney, rising swiftly and with one hand pressing Brennan down to prevent him from rising also.

"All objections are overruled. The new Ward of the State will meet with me in my chambers at once. Court is adjourned."

The session was stormy but brief. Holden objected to everything, but the voice of Judge Carter was loud and his stature was large; they overrode James Holden and compelled his attention.

"We're out of the court," snapped Judge Carter. "We no longer need observe the niceties of court etiquette, so now shut up and listen! Holden, you are involved in a thing that is explosively dangerous. You claim it to be a secret, but your secret is slowly leaking out of your control. You asked for your legal competence to be ruled. Fine, but if I allowed that, every statement made by you about your education would be in court record and your so-called secret that much more widespread. How long do you think it would have been before millions of people howled at your door? Some of them yelping for help and some of them bitterly objecting to tampering with the immature brain? You'd be accused of brainwashing, of making monsters, of depriving children of their heritage of happiness—and in the same ungodly howl there would be ve̶r̶y̶ ̶l̶o̶u̶d̶l̶y̶ damning you for not tossing your process into their laps. And there would be a number trying to get to you on the sly so that they could get a head start over the rest.

"You want your competence affirmed legally? James, you have not the stature nor the voice to fight them off. Even now, your little secret is in danger and you'll probably have to bribe a few wiseacres with a touch of accelerated knowledge to keep them from spilling the whole story, even though I've ruled your testimony incompetent and immaterial and stricken from the record. Now, we'll study this system of yours under controlled conditions as your parents wanted, and we'll have professional help and educated advice, and both you and your process shall be under the protection of my Court, and when the time comes you shall receive the kudos and benefits from it. Understand?"

"Yes sir."

"Good. Now, as my first order, you go back to Shipmont and pack your gear. You'll report to my home as soon as you've made all the arrangements. There'll be no more hiding out and playing your little process in secret either from Paul Brennan—yes, I know that you believe that he was somehow instrumental in the death of your parents but have no shred of evidence that would stand in court—or the rest of the world. Is that, and everything else I've said in private, very clear?"

"Yes, sir."

"Good. Now, be off with you. And do not hesitate to call upon me if there is any interference whatsoever."

CHAPTER SIXTEEN

Judge Carter insisted and won his point that James Holden accept residence in his home.

He did not turn a hair when the trucks of equipment arrived from the house on Martin's Hill; he already had room for it in the cellar. He cheerfully allowed James the right to set it up and test it out. He respected James Holden's absolute insistence that no one be permitted to touch the special circuit that was the heart of the entire machine. Judge Carter also counter-requested—and enforced the request—that he be allowed to try the machinery out. He took a simple reading course in higher mathematics, after discovering that Holden's machine would not teach him how to play the violin. (Judge Carter already played the violin—but badly.)

Later, the judge committed to memory the entire book of Bartlett's Famous Quotations despite the objection of young Holden that he was cluttering up his memory with a lot of useless material. The Judge learned (as James had learned earlier) that the proper way to store such information in the memory was to read the book with the machine turned in "stand-by" until some section was encountered that was of interest. Using this method, the judge picked and pecked at the Holy Bible, a number of documents that looked like important governmental records, and a few books in modern history.

Then there came other men. First was a Professor Harold White from the State Board of Education

who came to study both Holden and Holden's
machinery and what it did. Next came a Dr. Persons
who said very little but made diagrams and histograms and graphs which he studied. The third was a
rather cheerful fellow called Jack Cowling who was
more interested in James Holden's personal feelings
than he was in the machine. He studied many subjects superficially and watched the behavior of young
Holden as Holden himself studied subjects recommended by Professor White.

White had a huge blackboard installed on the cellar wall opposite the machine, and he proceeded to
fill the board with block outlines filled with crabbed
writing and odd-looking symbols. The whole was
meaningless to James Holden; it looked like the organization chart of a large corporation but it contained no names or titles. The arrival of each new
visitor caused changes in the block diagram.

These arrivals went at their project with stop
watches and slide rules. They calibrated themselves
and James with the cold-blooded attitude of racetrack
touts clocking their favorite horses. Where James had
simply taken what he wanted or what he could at any
single sitting, then let it settle in his mind before taking another dose of unpremeditated magnitude, these
fellows ascertained the best effectiveness of each application to each of them. They tried taking long
terms under the machine and then they measured the
time it took for the installed information to sink in
and settle into usable shape. Then they tried shorter
and shorter sittings and measured the correspondingly
shorter settling times. They found out that no two
men were alike, nor were any two subjects. They discovered that a man with an extensive education already could take a larger sitting and have the new
information available for mental use in a shorter settling time than a man whose education had been
sketchy or incomplete.

They brought in men who had either little or no

mathematics and gave them courses in advanced subjects. Afterwards they provided the foundation mathematics and they calibrated and measured the time it took for the higher subject to be understood as it aligned its information to the whole. Men came with crude English and bluntly read the dictionary and the proper rules of grammar and they were checked to see if their early bad-speech habits were corrected, and to what degree the Holden machine could be made to help repair the damage of a lifelong ingrained set of errors. They sent some of these boys through comparison dictionaries in foreign tongues and then had their language checked by specialists who were truly polylingual. There were some who spoke fluent English but no other tongue; these progressed into German with a German-to-English comparison dictionary, and then into French via a German-to-French comparison and were finally checked out in French by French-speaking examiners.

And Professor White's block diagram grew complex, and Dr. Persons's histograms filled pages and pages of his broad notebooks.

It was the first time that James Holden had ever seen a team of researchers plow into a problem, running a cold and icy scientific investigation to ascertain precisely how much cause produced how much effect. Holden, who had taken what he wanted or needed as the time came, began to understand the desirability of full and careful programming. The whole affair intrigued him and interested him. He plunged in with a will and gave them all the help he could.

He had no time to be bored, and he did not mark the passage of time until he arrived at his thirteenth birthday.

Then one night shortly after his birthday, James Holden discovered women indirectly. He had his first erotic dream.

We shall not go into the details of this midnight introduction to the arrival of manhood, for the simple reason that if we dwell on the subject, someone is certain to attempt a dream-analysis and come up with some flanged-up character-study or personality-quirk that really has nothing to do with the mind or body of James Holden. The truth is that his erotic dream was pleasantly stirring, but not entirely satisfactory. It was fun while it lasted, but it didn't last very long. It awakened him to the realization that knowledge is not the end-all of life, and that a full understanding of the words, the medical terms, and the biology involved did not tell him a thing about this primary drive of all life.

His total grasp of even the sideline issues was still dim. He came to a partial understanding of why Jake Caslow had entertained late visitors of the opposite sex, but he still could not quite see the reason why Jake kept the collection of calendar photographs and paintings hung up around the place. Crude jokes and rude talk heard long years before and dimly remembered did not have much connection with the subject. To James Holden, a "tomato" was still a vegetable, although he knew that some botanists were willing to argue that the tomato was really a fruit.

For many days he watched Judge Carter and his wife with a critical curiosity that their childless life had never known before. James found that they did not act as if something new and strangely thrilling had just hit the known universe. He felt that they should know about it. Despite the fact that he knew everything that his textbooks could tell him about sex and copulation he still had the quaint notion that the reason why Judge Carter and his wife were childless was because they had not yet gotten around to Doing It. He made no attempt to correlate this oddity with its opposite in Jake Caslow's ladies of the night who seemed to go on their merry way without conceiving.

He remembered the joking parry-and-thrust of that midnight talk between Tim Fisher and Janet Bagley but it made no sense to him still. But as he pondered the multitude of puzzlements, some of the answers fell partly into place just as some of the matching pieces of a jigsaw puzzle may lie close to one another when they are dumped out of the box. Very dimly James began to realize that this sort of thing was not New, but to the contrary it had been going on for a long, long time. So long in fact that neither Tim Fisher nor Janet Bagley had found it necessary to state desire and raise objection respectively in simple clear sentences containing subject, verb, and object. This much came to him and it bothered him even more, now that he understood that they were bandying their meanings lightly over a subject so vital, so important, so—so completely personal.

Then, in that oddly irrational corner of his brain that neither knowledge nor information had been adequate to rationalize nor had experience arrived to supply the explanation, James Holden's limited but growing comprehension arrived at a conclusion that was reasonable within its limited framework. Judge Carter and his wife occupied separate bedrooms and had therefore never Done It. Conversely, Tim and Janet Fisher from their midnight discussion obviously Knew What It Was All About. James wondered whether they had Done It yet, and he also wondered whether he could tell by listening to their discussions and conversations now that they'd been married at least long enough to have Tried It.

With a brand new and very interesting subject to study, James lost interest in the program of concentrated research. James Holden found that all he had to do to arrange a trip to Shipmont was to state his desire to go and the length of his visit. The judge deemed both reasonable, Mrs. Carter packed James a bag, and off he went.

The house on Martin's Hill was about the same, with some improvement such as a coat of paint and some needed repair work. The grounds had been worked over, but it was going to take a number of years of concentrated gardening to de-weed the tangled lawn and to cut the undergrowth in the thin woodsy back area where James had played in concealment.

But the air inside was changed. Janet, as Mrs. Bagley, had been as close to James Holden as any substitute mother could have been. Now she seemed preoccupied and too busy with her own life to act more than pleasantly polite. He could have been visiting the home of a friend instead of returning to the domicile he had created, in which he had provided her with a home for herself and a frightened little girl. She asked him how he had been and what he was doing, but he felt that this was more a matter of taking up time than real interest. He had the feeling that somewhere deep inside, her soul was biting its fingernails. She spoke of Martha with pride and hope, she asked how Judge Carter was making out and whether Martha would be able to finish her schooling via Holden's machine.

James believed this was her problem. Martha had been educated far beyond her years. She could no more enter school now than he could; unwittingly he'd made Martha a misfit, too. So James tried to explain that part of the study undertaken in Judge Carter's program had been the question of what to do about Martha.

The professionals studying the case did not know yet whether Martha would remain ahead of her age group, or whether to let her loaf it out until her age group caught up with her, or whether to give Martha everything she could take as fast as she could take it. This would make a female counterpart of James Holden to study.

But knowing that there were a number of very brilliant scientists, educators, and psychologists working on Martha's problem did not cheer up Mrs. Janet Fisher as much as James thought it should. Yet as he watched her, he could not say that Tim Fisher's wife was *unhappy*.

Tim, on the other hand, looked fine. James watched them together as critically curious as he'd been in watching the Judge and Mrs. Carter. Tim was gentle with his wife, tender, polite, and more than willing to wait on her. From their talk and chit-chat, James could detect nothing. There were still elisions, questions answered with a half-phrase, comments added with a disconnected word and replied in another word that—in cold print—would appear to have no bearing on the original subject. This sort of thing told James nothing. Judge Carter and his wife did the same; if there were any difference to be noted it was only in the basic subject materials. The judge and his wife were inclined more toward discussions of political questions and judicial problems, whereas Tim and Janet Fisher were more interested in music, movies, and the general trend of the automobile repair business; or more to the point, whether to expand the present facility in Shipmont, to open another branch elsewhere, or to sell out to buy a really big operation in some sizable city.

James saw a change in Martha, too. It had been months since he came back home to supervise the removal of his belongings. Now Martha had filled out. She was dressed in a shirt-and-skirt instead of the little jumper dresses James remembered. Martha's hair was lightly wavy instead of trimmed short, and she was wearing a very faint touch of color on her lips. She wore tiny slippers with heels just a trifle higher than the altitude recommended for a girl close to thirteen.

Ultimately they fell into animated chatter of their own, just as they always had. There was a barrier between the pair of them and Martha's mother and stepfather—slightly higher than the usual barrier erected between children and their adults because of their educational adventures together. They had covered reams and volumes together. Martha's mother was interested in Holden's machine only when something specific came to her attention that she did not wish to forget such as a recipe or a pattern, and one very extensive course that enabled her to add a column of three-digit numbers by the whole lines instead of taking each column digit by digit. Tim Fisher himself had deeper interests, but nearly all of them directed at making Tim Fisher a better manager of the automobile repair business. There had been some discussion of the possibility that Tim Fisher might memorize some subject such as the names of all baseball players and their yearly and lifetime scoring, fielding, and playing averages, training for him to go as a contestant on one of the big money giveaway shows. This never came to pass; Tim Fisher did not have any spectacular qualities about him that would land him an invitation. So Tim's work with Holden's machine had been straightforward studies in mechanics and bookkeeping and business management—plus a fine repertoire of bawdy songs he had rung in on the sly and subsequently used at parties.

James and Martha had taken all they wanted of education and available information, sometimes with plan and the guidance of schoolbooks and sometimes simply because they found the subject of interest. In the past they'd had discussions of problems in understanding; they'd talked of things that parents and elders would have considered utterly impossible to discuss with young minds. With this communion of interests, they fell back into their former pattern of first joining the general conversation politely and then gradually confining their remarks to one another until there were two conversations going on at the same time, one between James and Martha and another between Janet and Tim. Again, the vocal interference and cross-talk became too high, and it was Tim and Janet who left the living room to mix a couple of highballs and start dinner.

The chatter continued, but now with a growing strain on the part of young James Holden.

He wanted to switch to a more personal topic of conversation but he did not know how to accomplish this feat. There was plenty of interest but it was more clinical than passionate; he was not stirred to yearning, he felt no overwhelming desire to hold Martha's hand nor to feel the softness of her face, yet there was a stirring urge to make some form of contact. But he had no·idea of how to steer the conversation towards personal lines that might lead into something that would justify a gesture towards her. It began to work on him. The original clinical urge to touch her just to see what reaction would obtain changed into a personal urge that grew higher as he found that he could not kick the conversational ball in that direction. The idea of putting an arm about her waist as he had seen men embrace their girls on television was a pleasing thought; he wanted to find out if kissing was as much fun as it was made up to be.

But instead of offering him any encouragement, or even giving him a chance to start shifting the conversation, Martha went prattling on and on and on about a book she'd read recently.

It did not occur to James Holden that Martha Bagley might entertain the idea of physical contact of some mild sort on an experimental basis. He did not even consider the possibility that he might *start* her thinking about it. So instead of closing the distance between them like a gentle wolf, watching with sly calculation to ascertain whether her response was positive, negative, or completely neutral, he sat like a post and fretted inwardly because he couldn't control the direction of their conversation.

Ultimately, of course, Martha ran out of comment on her book and then there fell a deadly silence because James couldn't dredge up another lively subject. Desperately, he searched through his mind for an opening. There was none. The bright patter between male and female characters in books he'd smuggled started off on too high a level on both sides. Books that were written adequately for his understanding of this problem signed off with the trite explanation that they lived happily ever afterwards but did not say a darned thing about how they went about it. The slightly lurid books that he'd bought, delivered in plain wrappers, gave some very illuminating descriptions of the art or act, but the affair opened with the scene all set and the principal characters both ready, willing, and able. There was no conversational road map that showed the way that led two people from a calm and unemotional discussion into an area that might lead to something entirely else.

In silence, James Holden sat there sinking deeper and deeper into his own misery.

The more he thought about it, the farther he found himself from his desire. Later in the process, he knew, came a big barrier called "stealing a kiss," and James with his literal mind provided this game with an aggressor, a defender, and the final extraction by coercion or violence of the first osculatory contact. If the objective could be carried off without the defense repulsing the advance, the rest was supposed to come with less trouble. But here he was floundering before he began, let alone approaching the barrier that must be an even bigger problem.

Briefly he wished that it were Christmas, because at Christmas people hung up mistletoe. Mistletoe would not only provide an opening by custom and tradition, it also cut through this verbal morass of trying to lead up to the subject by the quick process of supplying the subject itself. But it was a long time before Christmas. James abandoned that ill-conceived idea and went on sinking deep and feeling miserable.

Then Martha's mother took James out of his misery by coming in to announce dinner. Regretfully, James sighed for his lost moments and helplessness, then got to his feet and held out a hand for Martha.

She put her hand in his and allowed him to lift her to her feet by pulling. The first contact did not stir him at all, though it was warm and pleasant. Once the pulling pressure was off, he continued to hold Martha's hand, tentatively and experimentally.

Then Janet Fisher showered shards of ice with a light laugh. "You two can stand there holding hands," she said. "But I'm going to eat it while it's on the table."

James Holden's hand opened with the swiftness of a reflex action, almost as fast as the wink of an eye at the flash of light or the body's jump at the crack of sound. Martha's hand did not drop because she, too, was holding his and did not let go abruptly. She giggled, gave his hand a little squeeze and said, "Let's go. I'm hungry too."

None of which solved James Holden's problem. But during dinner his personal problem slipped aside because he discovered another slight change in Janet Fisher's attitude. He puzzled over it quietly, but managed to eat without any apparent preoccupation. Dinner took about a half hour, after which they spent another fifteen minutes over coffee, with Janet refusing her second cup. She disappeared at the first shuffle of a foot under the table, while James and Martha resumed their years-old chore of clearing the table and tackling the dishwashing problem.

Alone in the kitchen, James asked Martha, "What's with your mother?"

"What do you mean, what's with her?"

"She's changed, somehow."

"In what way?"

"She seems sort of inner-thoughtful. Cheerful enough but as if something's bothering her that she can't stop."

"That all?"

"No," he went on. "She hiked upstairs like a shot

right after dinner was over. Tim raced after her. And
she said no to coffee."

"Oh, that. She's just a little upset in the middle."

"But why?"

"She's pregnant."

"Pregnant?"

"Sure. Can't you see?"

"Never occurred to me to look."

"Well, it's so," said Martha, scouring a coffee cup
with an exaggerated flourish. "And I'm going to have
a half-sibling."

"But look—"

"Don't *you* go getting upset," said Martha. "It's a
natural process that's been going on for hundreds of
thousands of years, you know."

"When?"

"Not for months," said Martha. "It just happened."

"Too bad she's unhappy."

"She's very happy. Both of them wanted it."

James considered this. He had never come across
Voltaire's observation that marriage is responsible for
the population because it provides the maximum opportunity with the maximum temptation. But it was
beginning to filter slowly into his brain that the ways
and means were always available and there was neither custom, tradition, nor biology that dictated a
waiting period or a time limit. It was a matter of
choice, and when two people want their baby, and
have no reason for not having their baby, it is silly to
wait.

"Why did they wait so long if they both want it?"

"Oh," replied Martha in a matter-of-fact voice,
"they've been working at it right along."

James thought some more. He'd come to see if he
could detect any difference between the behavior of
Judge and Mrs. Carter, and the behavior of Tim and
Janet Fisher. He saw little, other than the standard
differences that could be accounted for by age and
temperament. Tim and Janet did not really act as if

they'd Discovered Something New. Tim, he knew, was a bit more sweet and tender to Janet than he'd been before, but there was nothing startling in his behavior. If there were any difference as compared to their original antics, James knew that it was undoubtedly due to the fact that they didn't have to stand lollygagging in the hallway for two hours while Janet half-heartedly insisted that Tim go home. He went on to consider his original theory that the Carters were childless because they occupied separate bedrooms; by some sort of deduction he came to the conclusion that he was right, because Tim and Janet Fisher were making a baby and they slept in the same bedroom.

He went on in a whirl; maybe the Carters didn't want children, but it was more likely that they too had tried but it hadn't happened.

And then it came to him suddenly that here he was in the kitchen alone with Martha Bagley, discussing the very delicate subject. But he was actually no closer to his problem of becoming a participant than he'd been an hour ago in the living room. It was one thing to daydream the suggestion when you can also daydream the affirmative response, but it was another matter when the response was completely out of your control. James was not old enough in the ways of the world to even consider outright asking; even if he had considered it, he did not know how to ask.

The evening went slowly. Janet and Tim returned about the time the dishwashing process was complete. Janet proposed a hand of bridge; Tim suggested poker, James voted for pinochle, and Martha wanted to toss a coin between canasta or gin rummy. They settled it by dealing a shuffled deck face upward until the ace of hearts landed in front of Janet, whereupon they played bridge until about eleven o'clock. It was interesting bridge; James and Martha had studied bridge columns and books for recreation; against them were aligned Tim and Janet, who played with the card sense developed over years of practice. The youngsters knew the theories, their bidding was as precise as bridge bidding could be made with value-numbering, honor-counting, response-value addition, and all of the other systems. They understood all of the coups and end plays complete with classic examples. But having all of the theory engraved on their brains did not temporarily imprint the location of every card already played, whereas Tim and Janet counted their played cards automatically and made up in play what they missed in stratagem.

At eleven, Janet announced that she was tired, Tim joined her; James turned on the television set and he and Martha watched a ten-year-old movie for an hour. Finally Martha yawned.

And James, still floundering, mentally meandered back to his wish that it were Christmas so that mistletoe would provide a traditional gesture of affection, and came up with a new and novel idea that he expressed in a voice that almost trembled:

"Tired, Martha?"

"Uh-huh."

"Well, why don't I kiss you good night and send you off to bed."

"All right, if you want to."

"Why?"

"Oh—just—well, everybody does it."

She sat near him on the low divan, looking him full in the face but making no move, no gesture, no change in her expression. He looked at her and realized that he was not sure of how to take hold of her, how to reach for her, how to proceed.

She said, "Well, go ahead."

"I'm going to."

"When?"

"As soon as I get good and ready."

"Are we going to sit here all night?"

In its own way, it reminded James of the equally

un-brilliant conversation between Janet and Tim on the homecoming after their first date. He chuckled.

"What's so funny?"

"Nothing," he said in a slightly strained voice. "I'm thinking that here we sit like a couple of kids that don't know what it's all about."

"Well," said Martha, "aren't we?"

"Yes," he said reluctantly, "I guess we are. But darn it, Martha, how does a guy grow up? How does a guy learn these things?" His voice was plaintive, it galled him to admit that for all of his knowledge and his competence, he was still just a bit more than a child emotionally.

"I don't know," she said in a voice as plaintive as his. "I wouldn't know where to look to find it. I've tried. All I know," she said with a quickening voice, "is that somewhere between now and then I'll learn how to toss talk back and forth the way they do."

"Yes," he said glumly.

"James," said Martha brightly, "we should be somewhat better than a pair of kids who don't know what it's all about, shouldn't we?"

"That's what bothers me," he admitted. "We're neither of us stupid. Lord knows we've plenty of education between us, but—"

"James, how did we get that education?"

"Through my father's machine."

"No, you don't understand. What I mean is that no matter how we got our education, we had to learn, didn't we?"

"Why, yes. In a—"

"Now, let's not get involved in another philosophical argument. Let's run this one right on through to the end. Why are we sitting here fumbling? Because we haven't yet learned how to behave like adults."

"I suppose so. But it strikes me that anything should be—"

"James, for goodness' sake. Here we are, the two people in the whole world who have studied everything we know together, and when we hit something we can't study—you want to go home and kiss your old machine," she finished with a remarkable lack of serial logic. She laughed nervously.

"What's so darned funny?" he demanded sourly.

"Oh," she said, "you're afraid to kiss me because you don't know how, and I'm afraid to let you because I don't know how, and so we're talking away a golden opportunity to find out. James," she said seriously, "if you fumble a bit, I won't know the difference because I'm no smarter than you are."

She leaned forward holding her face up, her lips puckered forward in a tight little rosebud. She closed her eyes and waited. Gingerly and hesitantly he leaned forward and met her lips with a pucker of his own. It was a light contact, warm, and ended quickly with a characteristic smack that seemed to echo through the silent house. It had all of the emotional charge of a mother-in-law's peck, but it served its purpose admirably. They both opened their eyes and looked at one another from four inches of distance. Then they tried it again and their second was a little longer and a little warmer and a little closer, and it ended with less of the noise of opening a fruit jar.

Martha moved over close beside him and put her head on his shoulder; James responded by putting an arm around her, and together they tried to assemble themselves in the comfortably affectionate position seen in movies and on television. It didn't quite work that way. There seemed to be too many arms and legs and sharp corners for comfort, or when they found a contortion that did not create interferences with limb or corner, it was a strain on the spine or a twist in the neck. After a few minutes of this coeducational wrestling they decided almost without effort to return to the original routine of kissing. By more luck than good management they succeeded in an embrace that placed no strain and which met them almost face to face. They puckered again and made contact, then pressure came and spread out the pair of tightly pursed rosebuds. Martha moved once to get her nose free of his cheek for a breath of air.

At the rate they were going, they might have hit paydirt this time, but just at the point where James should have relaxed to enjoy the long kiss he began to worry: There is something planned and final about the quick smacking kiss, but how does one gracefully terminate the long-term, high-pressure jobs? So instead of enjoying himself, James planned and discarded plans until he decided that the way he'd do it would be to exert a short, heavy pressure and then cease with the same action as in the quick-smack variety.

It worked fine, but as he opened his eyes to look at her, she was there with her eyes still closed and her lips still ready. He took a deep breath and plunged in again. Having determined how to start, James was now going to experiment with endings.

They came up for air successfully again, and then spent some time wriggling around into another position. The figure-fitting went easier this time, after threshing around through three or four near-comforts they came to rest in a pleasantly natural position and James Holden became nervously aware of the fact that his right hand was cupped over a soft roundness that filled his palm almost perfectly. He wondered whether to remove it quickly to let her know that this intimacy wasn't intentional; slowly so that (maybe, he hoped) she wouldn't realize that it had been there; or to leave it there because it felt pleasant. While he was wondering, Martha moved around because she could not twist her neck all the way around like an owl, and she wanted to see him. The move solved his problem but presented the equally great problem of how he would try it again.

James allowed a small portion of his brain to think about this, and put the rest of his mind at ease by kissing her again. Halfway through, he felt warm moistness as her lips parted slightly, then the tip of her tongue darted forward between his lips to quest against his tongue in a caress so fleeting that it was withdrawn before he could react—and James reacted by jerking his head back faster than if he had been clubbed in the face. He was still tingling with the shock, a pleasant shock but none the less a shock, when Martha giggled lightly.

He bubbled and blurted, "Wha—whu—?"

She told him nervously, "I've been wanting to try that ever since I read it in a book."

He shivered. "What book?" he demanded in almost a quaver.

"A paperback of Tim's. Mother calls them, Tim's sex and slay stories." Martha giggled again. "You jumped."

"Sure did. I was surprised. Do it again."

"I don't think so."

"Didn't you like it?"

"Did you?"

"I don't know. I didn't have time to find out."

"Oh."

He kissed her again and waited. And waited. And waited. Finally he moved back an inch and said, "What's the matter?"

"I don't think we should. Maybe we ought to wait until we're older."

"Not fair," he complained. "You had all the warning."

"But—"

"Didn't you like it?" he asked.

"Well, it gave me the most tickly tingle."

"And all I got was a sort of mild electric shock. Come on."

"No."

"Well, then, I'll do it to you."

"All right. Just once."

Leaping to the end of this midnight research, there are three primary ways of concluding, namely: 1, physical satisfaction; 2, physical exhaustion; and 3, interruption. We need not go into sub-classifications or argue the point. James and Martha were not emotionally ready to conclude with mutual defloration. Ultimately they fell asleep on the divan with their arms around each other. They weren't interrupted; they awoke as the first flush of daylight brightened the sky, and with one more rather chaste kiss, they parted to fall into the deep slumber of complete physical and emotional exhaustion.

CHAPTER SEVENTEEN

James Holden's ride home on the train gave him a chance to think, alone and isolated from all but superficial interruptions. He felt that he was quite the bright young man.

He noticed with surreptitious pride that folks no longer eyed him with sly, amused, knowing smiles whenever he opened a newspaper. Perhaps some of their amusement had been the sight of a youngster struggling with a full-spread page, employing arms that did not quite make the span. But most of all he hated the condescending tolerance; their everlasting attitude that everything he did was "cute" like the little girl who decked herself out in mother's clothing from high heels and brassiere to evening gown, costume jewelry, and a fumbled smear of makeup.

That was over. He'd made it to a couple of months over fourteen, he'd finally reached a stature large enough so that he did not have to prove his right to buy a railroad ticket, nor climb on the suitcase bar so that he could peer over the counter. Newsdealers let him alone to pick his own fare instead of trying to "save his money" by shoving Mickey Mouse at him and putting his own choice back on its pile.

He had not succeeded in gaining his legal freedom, but as Ward of the State under Judge Carter he had other interesting expectations that he might not have stumbled upon. Carter had connections; there was talk of James' entering a comprehensive examination at some university, where the examining board,

forearmed with the truth about his education, would
test James to ascertain his true level of comprehension. He could of course collect his bachelor's degree
once he complied with the required work of term papers written to demonstrate that his information could
be interwoven into the formation of an opinion, or
reflection, or view of some topic. Master's degrees and
doctor's degrees required the presentation of some
original area of study, competence in his chosen field,
and the development of some facet of the field that
had not been touched before. These would require
more work, but could be handled in time.

In fact, he felt that he was in pretty good shape.
There were a couple of sticky problems, still. He
wanted Paul Brennan to get his comeuppance, but he
knew that there was no evidence available to support
his story about the slaughter of his parents. It galled
him to realize that cold-blooded, premeditated murder for personal profit and avarice could go undetect-
ed. But until there could be proffered some material
evidence, Brennan's word was as good as his in any
court. So Brennan was getting away with it.

The other little item was his own independence.
He wanted it. That he might continue living with
Judge Carter had no bearing. No matter how benevolent the tyranny, James wanted no part of it. In fighting for his freedom, James Holden's foot had slipped.
He'd used his father's machine on Martha, and that
was a legal error.

Martha? James was not really sorry he'd slipped.
Error or not, he'd made of her the only person in the
world who understood his problem wholly and sym-
pathetically. Otherwise he would be completely alone.

Oh yes, he felt that he was quite the bright young
man. He was coming along fine and getting somewhere. His very pleasant experiences in the house on
Martin's Hill had raised him from a boy to a young
man; he was now able to grasp the appreciation of
the Big Drive, to understand some of the reasons why

adults acted in the way that they did. He hadn't managed another late session of sofa with Martha, but there had been little incidental meetings in the hallway or in the kitchen with the exchange of kisses, and they'd boldly kissed goodbye at the railroad station under her mother's smile.

He could not know Janet Fisher's mind, of course. Janet, mother to a girl entering young womanhood, worried about all of the things that such a mother worries about and added a couple of things that no other mother ever had. She could hardly slip her daughter a smooth version of the birds and the bees and people when she knew full well that Martha had gone through a yard or so of books on the subject that covered everything from the advanced medical to the lurid exposé and from the salacious to the ribald. Janet could only hope that her daughter valued her chastity according to convention despite the natural human curiosity which in Martha would be multiplied by the girl's advanced education. Janet knew that young people were marrying younger and younger as the years went on; she saw young James Holden no longer as a rather odd youngster with abilities beyond his age. She saw him now as the potential mate for Martha. And when they embraced and kissed at the station, Janet did not realize that she was accepting this salute as the natural act of two sub-adults, rather than a pair of precocious kids.

At any rate, James Holden felt very good. Now he had a girl. He had acquired one more of the many attitudes of the Age of Maturity.

So James settled down to read his newspaper, and on page three he saw a photograph and an article that attracted his attention. The photograph was of a girl no more than seven years old holding a baby at least a year old. Beside them was a boy of about nine. In the background was a miserable hovel made of crude lumber and patched windows. This couple and their baby had been discovered by a geological survey outfit living in the backwoods hills. Relief, aid, and help were being rushed, and the legislature was considering ways and means of their schooling. Neither of them could read or write.

James read the article, and his first thought was to proffer his help. Aid and enlightenment they needed, and they needed it quickly. And then he stopped immediately because he could do nothing to educate them unless they already possessed the ability to read.

His second thought was one of dismay. His exultation came down with a dull thud. Within seconds he realized that the acquisition of a girl was no evidence of his competent maturity. The couple photographed were human beings, but intellectually they were no more than animals with a slight edge in vocabulary. It made James Holden sick at heart to read the article and to realize that such filth and ignorance could still go on. But it took a shock of such violence to make James realize that clams, guppies, worms, fleas, cats, dogs, and the great whales reproduced their kind; intellect, education and mature competence under law had nothing to do with the process whatsoever.

And while his heart was still unhappy, he turned to page four and read an open editorial that discussed the chances of The Educational Party in the coming Election Year.

James blinked.

"Splinter" parties, the editorial said, seldom succeeded in gaining a primary objective. They only succeeded in drawing votes from the other major parties, in splitting the total ballot, and dividing public opinion. On the other hand, they did provide a useful political weathervane for the major parties to watch most carefully. If the splinter party succeeded in capturing a large vote, it was an indication that the People found their program favorable and upon such evidence it behooved the major parties to mend their political fences—or to relocate them.

Education, said the editorial, was a primary issue and had been one for years. There had been experimenting with education ever since the Industrial Revolution uncovered the fact, in about 1900, that backbreaking physical toil was going to be replaced by educated workers operating machinery.

Then the editorial quoted Judge Norman L. Carter:

" 'For many years,' said Judge Carter, 'we have deplored the situation whereby a doctor or a physicist is not considered fully educated until he has reached his middle or even late twenties. Yet instead of speeding up the curriculum in the early school years, we have introduced such important studies as social graces, baton twirling, interpretive painting and dancing, and a lot of other fiddle-faddle which graduates students who cannot spell, nor read a book, nor count above ten without taking off their shoes. Perhaps such studies are necessary to make sound citizens and graceful companions. I shall not contest the point. However, I contend that a sound and basic schooling should be included—and when I so contend I am told by our great educators that the day is not long enough nor the years great enough to accomplish this very necessary end.

" 'Gentlemen, we leaders of The Education Party propose to accomplish precisely that which they said cannot be done!' "

The editorial closed with the terse suggestion: Educator—Educate thyself!

James Holden sat stunned.

What was Judge Carter doing?

James Holden arrived to find the home of Judge Norman L. Carter an upset madhouse. He was stopped at the front door by a secretary at a small desk whose purpose was to screen the visitors and to log them in and out in addition to being decorative. Above her left breast was a large enamelled button, red on top, white in the middle as a broad stripe from left to right, and blue below. Across the white stripe was printed CARTER in bold, black letters. From in back of the pin depended two broad silk ribbons that cascaded forward over the stuffing in her brassiere and hung free until they disappeared behind the edge of the desk. She eyed James with curiosity. "Young man, if you're looking for throwaways for your civics class, you'll have to wait until we're better organized—"

James eyed her with cold distaste. "I am James Quincy Holden," he told her, "and you have neither the authority nor the agility necessary to prevent my entrance."

"You are—I what?"

"I live here," he told her flatly. "Or didn't they provide you with this tidbit of vital statistic?"

Wheels rotated behind the girl's eyes somewhere, and memory cells linked into comprehension. "Oh! You're James."

"I said that first," he replied. "Where's Judge Carter?"

"He's in conference and cannot be disturbed."

"Your objection is overruled. I shall disturb him as soon as I find out precisely what has been going on."

He went on in through the short hallway and found audible confusion. Men in groups of two to four stood in corners talking in bedlam. There was a layer of blue smoke above their heads that broke into skirls as various individuals left one group to join another. Through this vocal mob scene James went veering from left to right to avoid the groupings. He stood with polite insolence directly in front of two men sitting on the stairs until they made room for his passage—still talking as he went between them. In his room, three were sitting on the bed and the chair holding glasses and, of course, smoking like the rest.

James dropped his overnight bag on a low stand and headed for his bathroom. One of the men caught sight of him and said, "Hey kid, scram!"

James looked at the man coldly. "You happen to be using my bedroom. You should be asking my permission to do so, or perhaps apologizing for not having asked me before you moved in. I have no intention of leaving."

"Get the likes of him!"

"Wait a moment, Pete. This is the Holden kid."

"The little genius, huh?"

James said, "I am no genius. I do happen to have an education that provides me with the right to criticize your social behavior. I will neither be insulted nor patronized."

"Listen to him, will you!"

James turned and with the supreme gesture of contempt, he left the door open.

He wound his way through the place to Judge Carter's study and home office, strode towards it with purpose and reached for the doorknob. A voice halted him: "Hey kid, you can't go in there!"

Turning to face the new voice, James said calmly, "You mean 'may not' which implies that I have asked your permission. Your statement is incorrect as phrased and erroneous when corrected."

He turned the knob and entered. Judge Carter sat at his desk with two men; their discussion ceased with the sound of the doorknob. The judge looked up in annoyance. "Hello, James. You shouldn't have come in here. We're busy. I'll let you know when I'm free."

"You'd better make time for me right now," said James angrily. "I'd like to know what's going on here."

"This much I'll tell you quickly. We're planning a political campaign. Now, please—"

"I know you're planning a political campaign," replied James. "But if you're proposing to campaign on the platform of a reform in education, I suggest that

you educate your henchmen in the rudimentary ele-
ments of polite speech and gentle behavior. I dislike
being ordered out of my room by usurpers who have
the temerity to address me as 'hey kid'."

"Relax, James. I'll send them out later."

"I'd suggest that you tell them off," snapped James.
He turned on his heel and left, heading for the cellar.
In the workshop he found Professor White and Jack
Cowling presiding over the machine. In the chair
with the headset on sat the crowning insult of all:

Paul Brennan leafing through a heavy sheaf of papers, reading and intoning the words of political ora-
tory.

Unable to lick them, Brennan had joined them—or,
wondered young Holden, was Judge Norman L. Carter paying for Brennan's silence with some plum of
political patronage?

As he stood there, the years of persecution rose
strong in the mind of James Holden. Brennan, the
man who'd got away with murder and would continue to get away with it because there was no shred
of evidence, no witness, nothing but James Holden's
knowledge of Brennan's actions when he'd thought
himself unseen in his calloused treatment of James
Holden's dying mother; Brennan's critical inspection
of the smashed body of his father, coldly checking the
dead flesh to be sure beyond doubt; the cruel search
about the scene of the 'accident' for James himself—
interrupted only by the arrival of a Samaritan, whose
name was never known to James Holden. In James
rose the violent resentment of the years, the certain
knowledge that any act of revenge upon Paul Brennan would be viewed as cold-blooded premeditated
murder without cause or motive.

And then came the angry knowledge that simple
slaughter was too good for Paul Brennan. He was not
a dog to be quickly released from misery by a merci-

ful death. Paul Brennan should suffer until he cried for death as a blessed release from daily living.

James Holden, angry, silently, unseen by the preoccupied workers, stole across the room to the main switch-panel, flipped up a small half-concealed cover, and flipped a small button.

There came a sharp *Crack!* that shattered the silence and re-echoed again and again through the room. The panel that held the repeater-circuit of the Holden Educator bulged outward; jets of smoke lanced out of broken metal, bulged corners, holes and skirled into little clouds that drifted upward—trailing a flowing billow of thick, black, pungent smoke that reached the low ceiling and spread outward, fanwise, obscuring the ceiling like a low-lying nimbus.

At the sound of the report, the man in the chair jumped as if he'd been stabbed where he sat.

"Ouyeowwww!" yowled Brennan in a pitiful ululation. He fell forward from the chair, asprawl on wobbly hands and knees, on elbows and knees as he tried to press away the torrent of agony that hammered back and forth from temple to temple. James watched Brennan with cold detachment, Professor White and Jack Cowling looked on in paralyzed horror. Slowly, oh, so slowly, Paul Brennan managed to squirm around until he was sitting on the floor still cradling his head between his hands.

James said, "I'm afraid that you're going to have a rough time whenever you hear the word 'entrenched'." And then, as Brennan made no response, James Holden went on, "Or were you by chance reading the word 'pedagogue'?"

At the word, Brennan howled again; the pain was too much for him and he toppled sidewise to writhe in kicking agony.

James smiled coldly, "I'm sorry that you weren't reading the word 'the'. The English language uses more of them than the word 'pedagogue'."

With remarkable effort, Brennan struggled to his

feet; he lurched toward James. "I'll teach you, you little—"

"Pedagogue?" asked James.

The shock rocked Brennan right to the floor again.

"Better sit there and think," said James coldly. "You come within a dozen yards of me and I'll say—"

"No! Don't!" screamed Paul Brennan. "Not again!"

"Now," asked James, "what's going on here?"

"He was memorizing a political speech," said Jack Cowling. "What did you do?"

"I merely fixed my machine so that it will not be used again."

"But you shouldn't have done that!"

"You shouldn't have been using it for this purpose," replied James. "It wasn't intended to further political ambitions."

"But Judge Carter—"

"Judge Carter doesn't own it," said James. "I do."

"I'm sure that Judge Carter can explain everything."

"Tell him so. Then add that if he'd bothered to give me the time of day, I'd be less angry. He's not to be interrupted, is he? I'm ordered out of my room, am I? Well, go tell the judge that his political campaign has been stopped by a fourteen-year-old boy who knows which button to push! I'll wait here."

Professor White took off; Jack Cowling smiled crookedly and shook his head at James. "You're a rash young man," he said. "What did you do to Brennan, here?"

James pointed at the smoke curling up out of the panel. "I put in a destructive charge to addle the circuit as a preventive measure against capture or use by unauthorized persons," he replied. "So I pushed the button just as Brennan was trying to memorize the word—"

"Don't!" cried Brennan in a pleading scream.

"You mean he's going to throw a fit every time he hears the word—"

"No! No! Can't anybody talk without saying—Ouwwouoooo!"

"Interesting," commented James. "It seems to start as soon as the fore-reading part of his mind predicts that the word may be next, or when he thinks about it."

"Do you mean that Brennan is going to be like the guy who could win the world if he sat on the top of a hill for one hour and did not think of the word 'Swordfish'? Except that he'll be out of pain so long as he doesn't think of the word—"

"Thing I'm interested in is that maybe our orator here doesn't know the definition thoroughly. Tell me, dear 'Uncle' Paul, does the word 'teacher' give—Sorry. I was just experimenting. Wasn't as bad as—"

Gritting his teeth and wincing with pain, Brennan said, "Stop it! Even the word 'sch-(wince)-ool' hurts like—" He thought for a moment and then went on with his voice rising to a pitiful howl of agony at the end: "Even the name 'Miss Adams' gives me a fleeting headache all over my body, and Miss Adams was on—ly—my—third—growww—school—Owuuuuoooo—teach—earrrrrr—Owwww!"

Brennan collapsed in his chair just as Judge Carter came in with his white mane flying and hot fire in his attitude. "What goes on here?" he stormed at James.

"I stopped your campaign."

"Now see here, you young—"

Judge Carter stopped abruptly, took a deep breath and calmed himself with a visible effort to control his rage. "James," he said in a quieter voice, "Can you repair the damage quickly?"

"Yes—but I won't."

"And why not?"

"Because one of the things my father taught me was the danger of allowing this machine to fall into the hands of ruthless men with political ambition."

"And I am a ruthless man with political ambition?"

James nodded. "Under the guise of studying me and my machine," he said, "you've been using it to train speakers and to educate ward-heelers. You've been building a political machine by buying delegates. Not with money, of course, because that is illegal. With knowledge, and because knowledge, education, and information are intangibles and no legality has been established, and this is all very legal."

Judge Carter smiled distantly. "It is bad to elevate the mind of the average ward-heeler? To provide the smalltime politician with a fine grasp of the National Problem and how his little local problems fit into the big picture? Is this making a better world, or isn't it?"

"It's making a political machine that can't be defeated."

"Think not? What makes you think it can't?"

"Pedagogue!" said James.

"Yeowwwww!"

The judge whirled to look at Brennan. "What was—that?" asked the judge.

James explained what had happened, then: "I've mentioned hazards. This is what would happen if a fuse blew in the middle of a course. Maybe he can be trained out of it, and maybe not. You'll have to try, of course. But think of what would happen if you and your political machine put these things into schools and fixed them to make a voltage twitch or something while the student was reading the word 're-publican'. You'd end up with a single-party system."

"And get myself assassinated by a group of righteously irate citizens," said Judge Carter. "Which I would very warmly deserve. On the other hand, suppose we 'treated' people to feel anguish at thoughts of murder or killing, theft, treason, and other forms of human deviltry?"

"Now that might be a fine idea."

"It would not," said Judge Carter flatly. James Holden's eyes widened, and he started to say something but the judge held up his hand, fingers outspread, and began to tick off his points finger by finger as he went on: "Where would we be in the case of enemy attack? Could our policemen aim their guns at a vicious criminal if they were conditioned against killing? Could our butchers operate; must our housewives live among a horde of flies? Theft? Well, it's harder to justify, James, but it would change the game of baseball as in 'stealing a base' or it would ruin the game of love as in 'stealing a kiss'. It would ruin the mystery-story field for millions of people who really haven't any inclination to go out and rob, steal, or kill. Treason? Our very revered Declaration of Independence is an article of Treason in the eyes of King George Third; it wouldn't be very hard to draw a charge of treason against a man who complained about the way the Government is being run. Now, one more angle, James. The threat or fear of punishment hasn't deterred any potential felon so far as anybody knows. And I hold the odd belief that if we removed the quart of mixed felony, chicanery, falsehood, and underhandedness from the human make-up, on that day the human race could step down to take its place alongside of the cow, just one step ahead of the worm.

"Now you accuse me of holding political ambition. I plead guilty of the charge and demand to be shown by my accuser just what is undesirable about ambition, be it political or otherwise. Have you no ambition? Of course you have. Ambition drove your folks to create this machine and ambition drove you to the fight for your freedom. Ambition is the catalyst that lifts a man above his fellows and then lifts them also. There is a sort of tradition in this country that a man must not openly seek the office of the Presidency. I consider this downright silly. I have announced my candidacy, and I intend to campaign for it as hard as I can. I propose to make the problem of *education* the most important argument that has ever come up in a presidential campaign. I believe that I shall win because I shall promise to provide this accelerated education for everybody who wants it."

"And to do this you've used my machine," objected James.

"Did you intend to keep it for yourself?" snapped Judge Carter.

"No, but—"

"And when did you intend to release it?"

"As soon as I could handle it myself."

"Oh, fine!" jeered the judge sourly. "Now, let me orate on that subject for a moment and then we'll get to the real meat of this argument. James, there is no way of delivering this machine to the public without delivering it to them through the hands of a capable Government agency. If you try to release it as an individual you'll be swamped with cries of anger and pleas for special consideration. The reactionaries will shout that we're moving too fast and the progressives will complain that we aren't moving fast enough. Teachers' organizations will say that we're throwing teachers out of jobs, and little petty politicians will try to slip their political plug into the daily course in Civics. Start your company and within a week some Madison Avenue advertising agency will be offering you several million dollars to let them convince people that Hickory-Chickory Coffee is the only stuff they can pour down their gullet without causing stomach pains, acid system, jittery nerves, sleepless nights, flat feet, upset glands, and so on and on and on. Announce it; the next day you'll have so many foreign spies in your bailiwick that you'll have to hire a stadium to hold them. You'll be ducking intercontinental ballistic missiles because there are people who would kill the dog in order to get rid of the fleas. You'll start the biggest war this planet has ever seen and it will go on long after you are killed and your father's secret is lost—and after the fallout has died off, we'll have another scientific race to re-create it. And don't think that it can't be rediscovered by determined scientists who know that such a thing as the Holden Electromechanical Educator is a reality."

"And how do you propose to prevent this war?"

"By broadcasting the secret as soon as we can; let the British and the French and the Russians and the Germans and all the rest build it and use it as wisely as they can program it. Which, by the way, James, brings us right back to James Quincy Holden, Martha Bagley, and the immediate future."

"Oh?"

"Yes. James, tell me after deliberation, at what point in your life did you first believe that you had the competence to enter the adult world in freedom to do as you believed right?"

"Um, about five or six, as I recall."

"What do you think now about those days?"

James shrugged. "I got along."

"Wasn't very well, was it?"

"No, but I was under a handicap, you know. I had to hide out."

"And now?"

"Well, if I had legal ruling, I wouldn't have to hide."

"Think you know everything you need to know to enter this adult world?"

"No man stops learning," parried James. "I think I know enough to start."

"James, no matter what you say, there is a very important but intangible thing called 'judgment'. You have part of it, but not by far enough. You've been studying the laws about ages and rights, James, but you've missed a couple of them because you've been looking for evidence favorable to your own argument. First, to become a duly elected member of the House of Representatives, a man must be at least twenty-five years of age. To be a Senator, he must be at least thirty. To be President, one must be at least thirty-five. Have you any idea why the framers of the

Constitution of the United States placed such restrictions?"

"Well, I suppose it had to do with judgment?" replied James reluctantly.

"That—and *experience*. Experience in knowing people, in understanding that there might be another side to any question, in realizing that you must not approach every problem from your own purely personal point of view nor expect it to be solved to your own private satisfaction or to your benefit. Now, let's step off a distance and take a good look at James Quincy Holden and see where he lacks the necessary ingredients."

"Yes, tell me," said James, sourly.

"Oh, I intend to. Let's take the statistics first. You're four-feet eleven-inches tall, you weigh one hundred and three pounds, and you're a few weeks over fourteen. I suppose you know that you've still got one more spurt of growth, sometimes known as the post-puberty-growth. You'll probably put on another foot in the next couple of years, spread out a bit across the shoulders, and that fuzz on your face will become a collection of bristles. I suppose you think that any man in this room can handle you simply because we're all larger than you are? Possibly true, and one of the reasons why we can't give you a ticket and let you proclaim yourself an adult. You can't carry the weight. But this isn't all. Your muscles and your bones aren't yet in equilibrium. I could find a man of age thirty who weighed one-oh-three and stood four-eleven. He could pick you up and spin you like a top on his forefinger just because his bones match his muscles nicely, and his nervous system and brain have had experience in driving the body he's living in."

"Could be, but what has all this to do with me? It does not affect the fact that I've been getting along in life."

"You get along. It isn't enough to 'get along.'

You've got to have judgment. You claim judgment, but still you realize that you can't handle your own machine. You can't even come to an equitable choice in selecting some agency to handle your machine. You can't decide upon a good outlet. You believe that proclaiming your legal competence will provide you with some mysterious protection against the wolves and thieves and ruthless men with political ambition—that this ruling will permit you to keep it to yourself until you decide that it is time to release it. You still want to hide. You want to use it until you are so far above and beyond the rest of the world that they can't catch up, once you give it to everybody. You now object to my plans and programs, still not knowing whether I intend to use it for good or for evil—and juvenile that you are, it must be good or evil and cannot be an in-between shade of gray. Men are heroes or villains to *you*; but *I* must say with some reluctance that the biggest crooks that ever held public office still passed laws that were beneficial to their people. There is the area in which you lack judgment, James. There and in your blindness."

"Blindness?"

"Blindness," repeated Judge Carter. "As Mark Twain once said, 'When I was seventeen, I was ashamed at the ignorance of my father, but by the time I was twenty-one I was amazed to discover how much the old man had learned in four short years!' Confound it, James, you don't yet realize that there are a lot of things in life that you can't even know about until you've lived through them. You're blind here, even though your life has been a solid case of encounter with unexpected experiences, one after the other as you grew. Oh, you're smart enough to know that you've got to top the next hill as soon as you've climbed this one, but you're not smart enough to realize that the next hill merely hides the one beyond, and that there are still higher hills beyond that stretching to the end of the road for you—and that when you've finally reached the end of your own road there will be more distant hills to climb for the folks that follow you.

"You've a fine education, and it's helped you tremendously. But you've loused up your own life and the life of Martha Bagley. You two are a pair of outcasts, and you'll be outcasts until about ten years from now when your body will have caught up with your mind so that you can join your contemporaries without being regarded as a pair of intellectual freaks."

"And what should I have done?" demanded James Holden angrily.

"That's just it, again. You do not now realize that there isn't anything you could have done, nor is there anything you can do now. That's why I'm taking over and I'm going to do it for you."

"Yes?"

"Yes!" snapped Judge Carter. "We'll let them have their courses in baton twirling and social grace and civic improvement and etiquette—and at the same time we'll give them history and mathematics and spelling and graduate them from 'high' school at the age of twelve or fourteen, introduce an intermediary school for languages and customs of other countries and in universal law and international affairs and economics, where our bookkeepers will learn science and scientists will understand commercial law; our lawyers will know business and our businessmen will be taught politics. After that we'll start them in college and run them as high as they can go, and our doctors will no longer go sour from the moment they leave school at thirty-five to hang out their shingle.

"As for you, James Holden, you and Martha Bagley will attend this preparatory school as soon as we can set it up. There will be no more of this argument about being as competent as an adult, because we old-sters will still be the chiefs and you kids will be the Indians. Have I made myself clear?"

"Yes sir. But how about Brennan?"

Judge Carter looked at the unhappy man. "You still want revenge? Won't he be punished enough just hearing the word 'pedagogue'?"

"For the love of—"

"Don't blaspheme," snapped the judge. "You'd hang if James could bring a shred of evidence, and I'd help him if I could." He turned to James Holden. "Now," he asked, "will you repair your machine?"

"And if I say No?"

"Can you stand the pressure of a whole world angered because you've denied them their right to an education?"

"I suppose not." He looked at Brennan, at Professor White and at Jack Cowling. "If I've got to trust somebody," he said reluctantly, "I suppose it might as well be you."

BOOK FOUR:
THE NEW MATURITY

CHAPTER EIGHTEEN

It is the campus of Holden Preparatory Academy.

It is spring, but many another spring must pass before the ambitious ivy climbs to smother the gray granite walls, before the stripling trees grow stately, before the lawn is sturdy enough to withstand the crab grass and the students. Anecdote and apocrypha have yet to evolve into hallowed tradition. The walks ways are bare of bronze plaques because there are no illustrious alumni to honor; Holden Preparatory has yet to graduate its first class.

It is youth, a lusty infant whose latent power is already great enough to move the world. As it rises, the world rises with it for the whole consists of all its parts; no man moves alone.

The movement has its supporters and its enemies, and between them lies a vast apathy of folks who simply don't give a damn. It supporters deplore the dolts and the sluggards who either cannot or will not be educated. Its enemies see it as a danger to their comfortable position of eminence and claim bitterly that the honored degree of doctor is being degraded. They refuse to see that it is not the degradation of the standard but rather the exaltation of the norm. Comfortable, they lazily object to the necessity of rising have no names, the circles have no statuary, the hall- alize that the ones who will be assaulting their fortress will themselves be fighting still stronger youth with the norm to keep their position. Nor do they re-one day when the mistakes are corrected and the program streamlined through experience.

On the virgin lawn, in a spot that will someday lie in the shade of a great oak, a group of students sit, sprawl, lie. The oldest of them is sixteen, and it is true that not one of them has any reverence for college degrees, because the entrance requirements demand the scholastic level of bachelor in the arts, the sciences, in language and literature. The mark of their progress is not stated in grades, but rather in the number of supplementary degrees for which they qualify. The honors of their graduation are noted by the number of doctorates they acquire. Their goal is the title of Scholar, without which they may not attend college for their ultimate education.

But they do not have the "look of eagles" nor do they act as if they felt some divine purpose fill their lives. They do not lead the pack in an easy lope, for who holds rank when admirals meet? They are not dedicated nor single-minded; if their jokes and pranks start on a higher or lower plane, it is just because they have better minds than their forebears at the same time.

On the fringe of this group, an olive-skinned Brazilian co-ed asks: "Where's Martha?"

John Philips looks up from a diagram of fieldmatrics he's been using to lay out a football play. "She's lending moral support to Holden. He's sweating out his scholar's impromptu this afternoon."

"Why should he be stewing?"

John Philips smiles knowingly. "Tony Dirk put the triple-whammy on him. Gimmicked up the random-choice selector in the Regent's office. Herr von James is discoursing on the subjects of Medicine, Astronomy, and Psychology—that is if Dirk knows his stuff."

Tony Dirk looks down from his study of a fluffy cloud. "Anybody care to hazard some loose change on my ability?"

"But why?"

"Oh," replies Philips, "we figure that the first graduating class could use a professional *Astrologer!* We'll be the first in history to have one—if M'sieu Holden can tie Medicine, Astronomy, and Psychology into something cogent in his impromptu."

It is a strange tongue they are using, probably the first birth-pains of a truly universal language. By some tacit agreement, personal questions are voiced in French, the reply in Spanish. Impersonal questions are Italian and the response in Portuguese. Anything of a scientific nature must be in German; law, language, or literature in English; art in Japanese; music in Greek; medicine in Latin; agriculture in Czech. Anything laudatory in Mandarin, derogatory in Sanskrit—and *ad libitum* at any point for any subject.

Anita Lowes has been trying to attract the attention of John Philips from his diagram long enough to invite her to the Spring Festival by reciting a low-voiced string of nuclear equations carefully compounded to make them sound naughty unless they're properly identified with full attention. She looks up and says, "What if he doesn't make the connection?"

Philips replies, "Well, if he can prove to that tough bunch that there is no possible advance in learning through a combination of Astronomy, Medicine, and Psychology, he'll make it on that basis. It's just as important to close a door as it is to open one, you know. But it's one rough deal to prove negation. Maybe we'll have James the Holden on our hands for another semester. Martha will like that."

"Talking about me?"

There is a rolling motion, sort of like a bushel of fish trying to leap back into the sea. The newcomer is Martha Fisher. At fifteen, her eyes are bright, and her features are beginning to soften into the beginning of a beauty that will deepen with maturity.

"James," says Tony Dirk. "We figured you'd like to have him around another four months. So we gimmicked him."

"You mean that test-trio?" chuckles Martha.

"How's he doing?"

"When I left, he was wriggling his way through probability math, showing the relationship between his three subjects and the solution for random choice figures which may or may not be shaded by known or not-known agency. He's covered Mason's History of Superstition and—"

"Superstition?" asks a Japanese.

Martha nods. "He claimed superstition is based upon fear and faith, and he feared that someone had tampered with his random choice of subjects, and he had faith that it was one of his buddies. So—"

Martha is interrupted by a shout. The years have done well by James Holden, too. He is a lithe sixteen. It is a long time since he formed his little theory of human pair-production and it is almost as long since he thought of it last. If he reconsiders it now, he does not recognize his part in it because everything looks different from within the circle. His world, like the organization of the Universe, is made up of schools containing classes of groups of clusters of sets of associations created by combinations and permutations of individuals.

"I made it!" he says.

James has his problems. Big ones. Shall he go to Harvard alone, or shall he go to coeducational California with the hope that Martha will follow him? Then there was the fun awaiting him at Heidelberg, the historic background of Pisa, the vigorous routine at Tokyo. As a Scholar, he has contributed original research in four or five fields to attain doctorates, now he is to pick a few allied fields, combine certain phases of them, and work for his Specific. It is James Holden's determination to prove that the son is worthy of the parents for which his school is named.

But there is high competition. At Carter tech-prep, a girl is struggling to arrange a Periodic Chart of the Nucleons. At Maxwell, one of his contemporaries will contend that the human spleen acts as an ion-ex-change organ to rid the human body of radioactive minerals, and he will someday die trying to prove it. His own classmate Tony Dirk will organize a weather-control program, and John Philips will write six lines of odd symbols that will be called the Inertiogravitic Equations.

Their children will reach the distant stars, and their children's children will, humanlike, cross the vast chasm that lies between one swirl of matter and the other before they have barely touched their home galaxy.

No man is an island, near or far on Earth as it is across the glowing clusters of galaxies—nay, as it may be in Heaven itself.

The motto is cut deep in the granite over the door-way to Holden Hall:

> YOU YOURSELF
> MUST LIGHT THE FAGGOTS
> THAT YOU HAVE BROUGHT